SUE JA JOO

Sue Ja Joo is a highly acclaimed novelist, poet, playwright, and visual artist. She spent 23 years living in France, Switzerland, and the U.S.A. Sue's literary inspiration comes from her deep roots in art, religion, and global cultures. She is at the frontier of the new literary genre called 'Smart Fiction' – a literary form between poetry and the short story. Sue Ja Joo was the first recipient of the Insung Park Literary Award for Mini-Fiction. She lives in Korea.

NIGHT
PICTURE
⊕
RAIN
SOUND

SEVENTEEN STORIES BY
SUE JA JOO

Translated by
Jennifer M. Cho

Edited by
Susan Blanshard

PAGE ADDIE PRESS
UNITED KINGDOM

Contents

To Heemin Kwon

The Burden Of Being Juliet

"Wait!" I exclaimed, desperately reaching for her hand. The piercing noise of my cries managed to plow through the fourth wall, right as Juliet was about to plunge a dagger into her heart. Surprised by my sudden interruption, she turned. Every fiber of my being told me this was a silence that needed to be broken. So I started, blurting out words without knowing quite what it was I needed to say.

"There, there, you're going way too far, th-this is such an over-reaction!"

The corner of her lips twitched. I took it as a cue to continue, my words rapid as bullets out a machine gun. After all, instead of singing sonnets, my generation spits the rhyming meters of rap.

"Why, oh why, would you do such a thing over … love?"

A perplexed expression fought across her face, as if to ask what else could possibly be as worthy as true love? I paused, frantically searching for a way to restructure my argument. I vaguely recalled the headlines I'd skimmed on suicide rates and moral responsibility.

"If you th-think about it … in society … it's like … an infectious disease … an epidemic!"

As I heard myself speak I realized I'd convince nobody. Perhaps a dose of philosophy would shine in my favor.

"Killing yourself over a guy, that just doesn't make sense … and really … does your death solve anything?"

What I really should have said was this: Romeo was head over heels in love with Rosaline yet forgot about her in a single night after laying eyes on you. He was in love with her much longer than he was with you … and you two were together for barely a week! As Friar Laurence said, "young men's love then lies, not truly in their hearts, but in their eyes." Do you truly believe the love of this Romeo guy is pure, sincere enough to sacrifice your life?

But, alas, my tongue twisted into the tightest of knots and I stood there, dumb. "Excuse me but who are you?"

So, she speaks! My eyes fixed on her plush pink lips. Sin-purging lips, with which I could easily fall in love.

"Ah … well … um … I'm just a reader. To be frank, I had to speak as I couldn't bear to see such beauty disappear this way. Besides, it doesn't seem fair to read a book and not be able to do anything about the story. A little one-sided, surely? If books can influence us, shouldn't readers be able to influence books as well?"

Juliet turned her back and looked away, as if she'd already decided to ignore my sophistries. To borrow some Shakespeare, she was like a ship, the sea, and the wind. Like the sea, her eyes could ebb and flow with tears. And her body was a ship sailing in a sea of saltwater tears. Her sighs were like a raging storm of wind. And she was on the verge of sinking to the depths of death.

"Hold on Juliet, please … just hold on!"

I grabbed her sleeve, desperate to stall this story arriving at its bitter denouement. My fingers grasped nothing but thin air. Was I dreaming? I looked down at my hands, which were gripping a small rectangular hardcover book. In it, Juliet was still alive.

"Perhaps living would be more painful than death itself. But we all take that pain and live on. We are all trapped, in a way, don't you think?"

I wasn't sure if I was making logical arguments or excuses – or perhaps both – but I knew I had to keep talking.

"I too have been in love, and out of love too, but really, it was all just a chapter in life, not the entire story … remember, this too shall pass, time can heal anything. Nothing lasts forever."

She didn't even blink. I continued to blabber on about past heartbreaks and, in my darkest moments, how even I had thoughts of ending everything. I divulged detail after detail, until my stories became as droll as white noise through the background.

Finally, while glancing at her lover's cold body Juliet spoke, in a calmly dignified tone as if she were talking down to her descendants.

"You speak of individual setbacks in life. The story of Romeo and me … it's different."

Her voice now thudded, gravity stricken, and she again pointed Romeo's dagger towards her heart. I wanted to shut my eyes, a child in denial. But I couldn't turn away.

"Our tale is not a simple love story … it is destined to remain as a symbol. A symbol of the sacrificed; a tale of the pure, innocent blood of two lambs. All to put an end to a febrile hatred between two households. You cannot change our destiny! And yet … how has our blighted tale become a love story to readers? It baffles me. Our story has been distorted, misrepresented. Just look: our entire world is built by symbols. We live within symbols, as symbols, and for symbols."

"What? Are you saying … life, death, love are all mere symbols? The world, as we know it, is not what it seems?"

Her words on how everything – the existence of people, the passing lives of those people, and the histories based on the lives of those people – was just symbol lingered by my side, then slapped me over the forehead. My mouth no longer blurted meaninglessnesses, and I stood there quietly, the book still in my hands, at a complete loss for words.

Appellations

"Apples, get your apples here!"

The fruit vendor shouted at the top of his lungs. He had a truck full of apples.

Picking one from the mound, he pulled a knife out of his pocket and proceeded to peel it. At the tip of his knife, the skin unraveled like a red ribbon, revealing the golden fruit in all its juicy splendor underneath.

"Mmmmmm – delicious! Ooooh – my mouth is watering. Ain't that true, kiddo?"

I wasn't quite a kid, but he certainly saw me that way. He looked down at me as if he were a giant, his eyes bulging like a pop-eyed goldfish. He then spun around and waved his hands in the air in a grand gesture, enunciating towards a non-existent audience.

"Fresh from the Garden of Eden itself! So sweet, so tempting! Taste the nectar that tempted poor Adam. Apples! Apples! Get 'em while you can!"

A woman appeared at my side, reaching tapered fingers out to select some apples. I recognized her, she and her husband were the newlyweds who lived upstairs. This modern-day Eve skimmed meticulously through the pile, silently estimating each apple's quality and worth. Her delicate fingers flipped the apples left and right as she scanned for bruises or other imperfections. All of a sudden, she brushed her hands over her apron and swiftly turned away.

"Pftt, it's not like they're cheaper than the store," she spat, and hurried away, disappearing into the shadows of the apartment building.

The fruit vendor's Adam's apple quivered. He held up his megaphone and shouted more loudly than before. I wondered if I should do something. Perhaps not.

"Apples! Crispy delicious! Sinfully sweet! Enough to bring down the blissful Adam and Eve!"

As he chanted, the vendor took two apples and tossed them high into the sky. The apples glided upwards, glistening under the sunlight, then began to fall. He caught them with ease, a juggling magician, and continued yammering. He shouted towards the playground. A few bored children came running. Their mothers followed. As his audience grew, the vendor increased his juggling act from two to three. Eyes, big and small, fixed towards the sky. He continued to add to the act – four, five, higher, even higher! Red apples spun and danced in the air. Jaws dropped in awe. With a triumphant smile, the vendor continued – toss, catch, toss, and catch.

In the blink of an eye, an apple deviated from its orbit. The rest followed, smashing to the ground.

"My, oh my, what do we have here? Could this be ... Sir Isaac

Newton's apple?" He nonchalantly tossed the smashed ones into a nearby bin.

"Pardon? You ask. Come again, you say! If it weren't for these apples, humans wouldn't have set foot on the moon. Thanks to these sorry saps splattered on the ground!"

The children dispersed. The juggling show was over, and no one was interested in a science lesson. The mothers and their purses followed. A woman with a foreign accent, perhaps a nanny, picked at the pile. She put the apples back, saying she didn't have enough money.

"Apples, apples! Easy on your wallet, tasty in your mouth! The clock is ticking, get 'em while you can!"

The Adam's Apple on the vendor's neck bulged again. I felt a tingle in my own throat and swallowed for no good reason.

"I've got 'em all, take your pick! Here's the very apple that William Tell shot off his son's head. How about the apple that put Snow White into the deepest of slumbers? Or an apple straight out of one of Cezanne's beautiful baskets? You want it, I've got it, I've got 'em all! Come one, come all, and walk away with the apple of your dreams! The clock is ticking, get 'em while you can!"

Words cascaded out of him like a waterfall. I heard him, certainly, but wasn't sure I was listening. A young man walked by the truck with a laptop under his arm. The vendor's eyes twinkled.

"Well, would you look at this … a computer from one of the biggest names in technology! Who loved apples you ask? Steve Jobs, of course. Your mama used to say that an apple a day keeps the doctor away? Well I say an apple a day can make you smart as the doctor, smart as Steve Jobs! Go ahead, buy your apples now, buy 'em while you can!" The vendor yelled into his megaphone, ping-ponging between the words "apple" and "smart." Before I knew it, eager mothers from the neighborhood emerged from their apartments. The vendor winked at me. The Mommy Mob surrounded him, cackling loudly, haggling fiercely. In the midst of the chaos, I slipped in between the cracks and swiped an apple. I turned and ran as fast as I could.

The apple in my hand felt smooth and silky to the touch. Its fresh scent tickled my nose. I opened my mouth wide as a hippopotamus, and took a ferocious bite. Crunch! As the golden flesh burst into my mouth, its sweet nectar tumbled across my tongue. Of all the apples in the world, with all the names that an apple could have been given, this one had entered my mouth. It was being consumed by me and, in this exact moment, had become a part of me. I couldn't help but smirk.

I had added yet another name to the long list, and felt a sense of accomplishment. It wasn't the most righteous name, but still it was a new one, an undeniable addition to the list. The stolen apple! I tried saying it out loud, but my mouth was full of fruit.

I munched with vigor, and felt a sudden shudder course down my spine. I spun around. The truck, and the vendor that had only moments ago stood alongside it, were no longer there. No longer could I see the Mommy Mob, nor the pile of apples that they had surrounded. Did they move to another alley? I searched left and right, but found nothing. Dazed and confused, I couldn't help but shrug, looking down at my half-eaten, stolen apple.

EMERGENCY CITY CLEAN-UP

The pitter-pattering of the rain called for a sense of urgency. Once it gets wet, trash becomes even more difficult to clean up. Why bother with cleaning in the rain? Without it, trash would clog the gutters, sewage would flow through the streets, and the detritus of a city's households would float like an aimless flotilla of boats across an endless urban sea. Not to mention the stench.

The people of the city go about their day without thinking of the trash that he maintains daily. Trash builds up regardless of the season; through the pollen-filled Spring breeze, in the excruciating summer heat, under the falling Autumn leaves, and amid the icy whirlwinds of Winter, one constant remains: the ever-present production of waste. This is why he was working with such fervor at dawn, in the rain, without complaint. He believed his work was a part of each day's cycle, that his efforts brought forth the day. One can laugh and say he was delusional or self-aggrandizing, but in truth nobody really knew him. All they knew was that he worked in the dark, organizing filth and grime.

The heightened humidity caused his body to sway vigorously. With each step he pierced through darkness, looking for his quarry. When he saw a piece of trash, he'd sweep it up. Some rubbish would disappear at the touch, as if a puff of smoke. He would look left and right, confused, and then see them taunting him on the large plasma TV screens hanging in the high-rise buildings above. Of course, he knew they would return to the streets once he turned his back. Some trash was just like that: simply too high for him to reach. Years of work had taught him so.

He looked around, finding himself in the middle of a ring of high-rise buildings. Indeed, it was intimidating. Each building looked down, like a tribe of Goliaths glaring at one small David. He wondered how each building had so many windows, and how each window would lead to a room that probably had trash in it as well. Would this trash from above be cleaner than the trash down here on the streets? Perhaps. The trash up there was probably just paper. Contracts, insurance documents, important sundry files muddled with deadlines and dollar signs. A single raindrop fell on his eyelid, reminding him to get on with the job, that he had little time for such wondering. He let out a sigh and returned his attention to the work at hand.

Every once in a while, he would spray the streets with salt, which worked best when cleaning up vomit from the night before. He didn't question why anyone would do such a thing, he just assumed that there were probably more than a few instances in life that would make one feel sick enough. Next to the puddles of spew he always found bottles. Everywhere, empty bottles filled the streets. He really couldn't understand how people would leave garbage that lasted forever just to satiate a moment's thirst. It was the latest epidemic. He shook his head, bitterly sweeping at the raindrops that fell beside him.

The rain continued, and its dampness weighed on him. He didn't care. Heavy rain would eventually clear up, just as piles of snow from a blizzard would eventually melt. Environmental crises would not solve themselves just because he worried about them. He was a nobody; just a lonely old broom. Back to work!

Out the corner of his eye he caught something odd. He looked closer … it wasn't just one. They were everywhere, stranded across the streets, piling up. Some were wrapped in newspaper and tossed aside like leftovers from yesterday's dinner. One could easily have passed by without noticing them. The more he looked, the more he found. There they were, in different hues and varying shapes. Most of them were various shades of red. He decided to touch one. Ugh! It was rotten and rock-hard. Disgusting. How were there so many, discarded as if trash? Did this mean some people possess more than one tongue? He had not realized there were so many of these in the streets. How could he not have noticed earlier?

After a few more blocks, he noticed other objects, which frightened him even more. Perhaps they had evolved from the trash, or perhaps they descended from the mighty high- rise buildings. He approached one, and poked it carefully. It was putrid, emitting a rancid smell. He looked closer … they were words, words that came with conflict. Fascism, Totalitarianism, Communism, Racism, Capitalism, and wedged between those words he found discarded curse words. These had already been used, as if bullets that had been fired — spent rounds.

How devastating, how gruesome, how pitiful. How ungrateful one must be to be born human, just to create such piles of weaponized garbage! He may be just a broom and in no place to judge, but he could not help but look down on those who had created those words, a systematic vocabulary that took hold of and shook this city upside down, words that brought an organized chaos to the world. He took hold of himself and returned to a calmer state of mind. After all, there was no use playing an endless blame game. He was given a job, and a very important job at that: he was to clean up this mess.

The rain had stopped. He continued to sweep against the asphalt, the broom's swooshing sound shifting to and fro. As daylight crept into the city, the streetlamps bowed and, one by one, flickered off. His surroundings were satisfyingly tidy, ready for the new day. Perhaps it would only last for a few minutes, but in that very moment the streets looked thoroughly kempt, almost like a young child's freshly combed hair. The darkness surrendered, and daylight filled the corners, bright as a theater set. At the last stroke of his sweeping, he looked up at his final destination. There he was, a simple broom that nobody cared for, at the end of another gruesome long shift, standing in front of City Hall.

Montage Of A Criminal

The sketch artist dug his hands deep into his pockets as he scurried down the slippery sidewalk on his way to the police station. It was definitely colder than the weather forecast had estimated. He glanced up towards the winter sky. Rain fell, no, it was snow… or was it sleet? He couldn't tell. The icy air swept across his nose, and the soles of his shoes made sloshing noises against the sidewalk's wet cobblestones. He hunched his shoulders, burrowing himself more deeply into his gray coat, and edged forward trying not to slip.

A part of him dreaded going to work, but he did it to hear the jangling sound of change in his pocket and keep silent the rumbling in his stomach for the next week or so. The job felt burdensome, sketching a model that you could see is easy, but conjuring criminal faces solely based off descriptions is a different game. He shuddered as he reached the station steps.

Opening the doors and looking around, he couldn't help but feel uneasy. Did the people of the station see his messy hair and ragged coat, and mistake him as a criminal? He looked at the men lining the hallway. A guy growled at him and spat on the floor, while another looked like he was ready to punch somebody square in the jaw. The sketch artist could not tell whether the men were crooks or cops, but he dared not take a closer look. He pulled two graphite drawing pencils from his shirt pocket and gripped them tightly, ready to defend himself. He picked his way cautiously through the crowded noisy hallway, and finally reached the detective's desk.

The detective was a complicated man. He had the temper of a tiger with the eyes of a hawk and, when he spoke, he snorted like an excited horse. Next to him the sketch artist felt small, with his hunched back and delicate neck extended as if always ready to retract back into a shell. The sketch artist scanned the desk with giraffe-like eyes, before meeting the detective's piercing gaze. The cop shouted at the sight of the sketch artist, his thunderous voice booming across the station.

"Damnit, that perv can go to hell!"

Startled, the sketch artist almost missed his chair as he sat down.

"What's the matter? Get yourself together man! Listen, this one we got today, he's a vicious little cockroach, I tell ya. Snatching hookers off the streets and having his way! We gotta get these guys and show 'em who's boss, y'know? Clean up the streets good so that old ladies, mothers, our daughters can safely move about town without a care. That's what we work for, day and night. These guys put the dinners on my table! You and I, we're gonna get screw-ups like these off the streets, so I need you to get your little sketch pad thingy out and focus!"

Nobody could recall the suspect's face, not even the one victim that'd survived the attack. Each said they remembered only vague images. The sketch artist sighed. It was depressing to think that after a life-or-death ordeal, all one was left with was a single, fleeting image. Would the only memory for him at his very last breath be a vague, blurry picture? And what would it be? The sketch artist shook his head. He'd have to finish the sketch by the weekend at the latest, for it would be distributed across the country's train stations, post offices, highway stops, and public buildings.

"Alright, let's start with the eyes!" the detective boomed.

The sketch artist would need to draw an identifiable, one-of-a-kind face. He valiantly picked up his battle weapons: drawing pencil in his right hand, eraser in the left.

"Yeah, so this guy had tiny, muddy eyes, just screaming 'filthy' all over, if you know what I mean. What, you don't? Speak up a bit will ya? I can barely hear you squeakin' there, man. Okay okay I got it, draw narrow eyes slanted to the side. We can fix it later if it doesn't look right, each one said the eyes looked real freaky."

The sketch artist's slender fingers moved with delicacy and accuracy. A couple of quick strokes later, and two beady eyes appeared on paper. The two men glared back at them, as if they were in a staring contest, and nodded at each other with approval.

"Moving on! According to these notes, he has a wide, square jawline … chubby cheeks … ha, well I wouldn't really trust the word of some of these people, if you know what I mean, but I guess this is what we've got … you gotta admit though, those ladies do sometimes have the intuition to scope out one sorry fucker after another. That gut instinct…"

The detective smirked, swearing further under his breath.

The sketch artist looked away without a word. He knew from experience that those were the women who offered comforts to the overlooked men of the city: they endured the gruesome, mothered the juvenile, and accepted any man judgement-free. Where else would the outcasts and failures go to seek affection and a moment's solace?

"Our little perp apparently has smaller nostrils, with the tip of his nose bent over like a hook!"

"Like … yours, Detective?"

This was a mistake. The detective's face turned beet red, and he started to huff like a wild horse at full gallop across a field. The sketch artist's heartbeat instantly elevated and he felt like a deer caught in headlights. At that moment the door swung open, and the detective's assistant popped his head in, asking if he had been summonsed. Alongside him entered the babbling noise from outside the office, pouring into the room and breaking the tension. The detective took his empty coffee mug and spat out a wad of phlegm, never removing his glaring eyes from the sketch artist, who was now anxiously chewing at the end of his pencil.

"What else do we have here … ah, ears, huge ears! They're round and sort of floppy, but sticking out like antennae!"

Looking at his notes, the detective chuckled. Then he paused, and took his hands slowly to his own ears, feeling their shape.

"The only weird thing, the one I don't get at all, is that his mouth doesn't look y'know … mean or nothin' … you wouldn't even think that this kid could swipe a pack of gum if you looked at his lips alone. They all said his lips were smooth, never chapped or dry. Well, I guess if he was droolin' over ladies nonstop, that pretty much explains that … okay, I think I've painted you a picture, enough talkin' now, more drawin'. You can look over this stuff if you need more."

The detective pushed forward a pile of folders containing victim's statements, along with recorded video footage showing pixelated blob-like images from some of the crimes. The sketch artist focused on piecing the puzzle together, using every fiber of his analytical gaze and, where that failed, sheer intuition. Beads of sweat formed on his forehead and crept down the nape of his neck, and the only sounds that filled the room now were the ticking clock and the stroke, stroke, stroke of his pencil. Finally, the sketch artist pushed his masterpiece towards the detective.

"What's this crap. I can't use this! That could be your regular Joe Schmo. I put this out and we'll get a hundred calls from a hundred different people within the hour."

The sketch artist was too taken aback to hear the detective's comments. He narrowed his eyes and looked at the sketch again. He couldn't disagree, and so he ripped the sketch to pieces, then tossed it in the bin next to the detective's desk. It always took more than a single draft to draw a criminal sketch. Especially when it was a common face.

Annoyed with himself, he grabbed a cigarette, pursing it between his lips, and leaned against the windowsill. He looked outside the window down at the street, where the common faces of the city roamed. It was still raining, no, it was snowing … or was it both? He really couldn't tell.

Where To Now, My Love?

Amid the sea of people swarming down the escalators towards the Orange Line, the woman looked up, double-checking whether she was at the right stop. Seoul National University of Education. She took a deep breath and started to make her way through the crowd. In the distance, she could hear the train coming. She would have to run.

At the same time she heard muffled, familiar ringtone. She fished her phone from the deepest recesses of her much too large purse, and put the phone to her ear.

"You're on your way, right?" "Yeah, I just got on the train."

The train carriage reeked of the morning's affairs: the faint, musty scent of an old dress that had just come out of the wardrobe; the stench of sweat that desperately needed to be erased under a hot shower; the smell of far too much hair product. Taken as an amalgam, it was suffocating. Her phone rang again. She felt an urge to whisper and shout at the same time.

"Hey sweetie, is that you?"

She could hear his peaceful, lazy voice on the other end.

"I was just saying, when you get to King's Palace Station, take

Exit 7."

"Got it."

The train stopped, and a horde of people stepped off. Now that she was no longer crammed between the shoulders of strangers, she could finally see the station sign through the window: Central Station. She could also see an empty seat. She made her way towards the seat, excited at the opportunity to sit down and relax for the remainder of her journey. Her phone, which she had switched to silent mode, started vibrating. She rummaged through her purse again. While swearing she'd keep her purse more organized in future and fastening her grip around the erstwhile phone, an elderly lady sat down triumphantly in the empty seat. The woman stopped in her tracks. She could hear the man chuckling through the phone.

"Oh, I guess I told you the wrong exit. It's exit number 4, not 7. My bad!"

She groaned and hung up before he could continue. It had been 18 minutes since she had left the University of Education Station. The subway had emerged from the subterranean dark and into sunlight, and they glided over the bridge above the Han River, which sparkled. From the corner of her eye, she caught a glimpse of the river's deathly dark shadows, where the sun hadn't yet reached. What a difference sunlight could make.

A cool breeze hit the nape of her neck as crowds ebbed at City Square Station. A chattering group shoved their way busily out of the station, fired up for action. In the city square tonight there was going to be another candlelit political protest. The woman felt relieved she was in the subway, not stuck in traffic on the road. She glanced up at the subway map above the doors. Two more stops.

As she finally stepped off the train onto the platform of King's Palace Station, she pulled out her phone and moved her lips like a goldfish gasping for air.

"Hey sweetie, I just got here."

"About time. Make sure to check the exit number on your way out." "You know I'm not a seven-year-old, right?"

"I'm just saying. Knowing you, if you take the wrong exit, it'll take forever to find your way back."

"Yeah yeah … what about after-"

The woman got cut off as a burly man rammed her shoulder. As she shook off the shock and pulled herself together, the man disappeared into the crowd. She could feel her blood boil.

"Did you find exit number 4?"

"I told you, I found the goddamn exit!"

"Whoa, what's with the attitude?"

She deliberated over whether she should just hang up and go home or not. She wasn't in the mood to be with a man who wouldn't listen.

"Are you there? Hello?"

"I'm still here. Stop being such a nag!"

"A nag? And here was, thinking I was being considerate, since somebody is always getting lost …"

He paused. He was probably distracted looking through his news-feed.

"Did you find the exit? It's next to the elevator. The stairs should be on the other side. There are quite a lot of stairs there. I think I read somewhere that there are more than 108 steps at this station. Come up that way."

"Could you be any more micro-managerial?"

"Hey, again, I'm just saying, this is all for you. If you're just going to bitch about it, let's just call it a day."

"Oh yeah? You read my mind!"

The woman angrily hit the red button on her phone's screen, ending the call. Who the hell did he think he was? She turned around and made her way back down the stairs. She held her phone tight in her hand so she wouldn't drop it or, perhaps, miss a call. She walked down the corridor that she had so busily hurried up a moment ago. She didn't remember it being so long. As she reached for the turnstile, she felt as if she heard her phone ring. She immediately looked down. Nothing. She had forgotten that her phone was on silent mode.

She paused. Then turned around, yet again. She must have been in the middle point of the 108 steps of the staircase. As she started to climb the stairs again, she twisted her ankle. As she looked left and right, the sheer amount of embarrassment masked her pain. Nobody was there. She took her right shoe off. The heel had broken and was hanging by a nail. Her phone rang again.

"Did you seriously hang up on me?"

"You were the one who wanted to call it a day." "You were the one who hung up."

"Does that really matter?"

"Where are you? Did you find Exit 4?"

She didn't bother explaining about her broken heel. Wedging her phone between her ear and shoulder, she looked through her purse and found a roll of scotch tape. Thank god for never organizing her purse. She grabbed her shoe and banged the heel against the floor. With a few swift motions, the heel stuck back into place. She secured the heel with tape. It wasn't going to be featured in Vogue anytime soon, but it would do for now. She let out a sigh of relief.

"Hmmm, where should I go now?"

"Once you take the exit, turn right. Go straight down, until you come to the crosswalk and make a left. Oh, as soon as you exit, there's a little hole-in-the-wall deli there. Why don't you pick up two ice-cream cones? I've suddenly got a hankering for vanilla. Yeah, so get two ice-cream cones, go straight down and make a left at the crosswalk. And hurry before the ice-cream melts!"

"Fine. How much longer after I make the left?"

Her newly fixed heel started to wobble. She stopped to make adjustments before continuing up the staircase.

"About 5 minutes?"

"Isn't that the President's residence?"

"No, no, no, if you see the residence, you've gone too far. It's only about a hundred meters."

The woman walked through Exit 4. It took a second for her eyes to adjust to the sun's sudden rays. As she stepped forward, her heel snapped off again and she tripped over the last step, falling forward onto the hot asphalt. Her purse also fell, spilling its contents. Coin purse, the lipstick she had been looking for that morning, her makeup kit, all scattered in separate directions. As she rushed to gather her things, the woman wondered if the situation could possibly get worse, and her sleeve brushed against her left eye, knocking out a contact lens. She squinted, shutting her unlensed eye, and felt around the ground in a forlorn hope of finding the missing contact. Nothing. She gave up, crawling across the ground to gather up the other belongings.

When she stood, finally, the throbbing in her ankle caught up with her. The pain bothered her more than the fact that she could barely see. She squinted towards the station exit, where busy people were briskly walking in their busy ways, paying no attention to her. What a relief. As another wave of people emerged from the station exit, she dusted herself off and applied the lipstick she had managed to find.

She walked into the tiny deli and paid for two vanilla flavored ice-cream cones. She took a right and then a left, hobbling the remaining hundred meters. Ice-creams in her right hand, and her broken shoe in the left, she realized she didn't have a hand to wipe the sweat dripping down her forehead. She would need to hurry, before the ice-cream melted.

From a distance, she could see a blurred shape she guessed might be him, enjoying a cigarette as he leaned against the palace gate, seeking shade from the blazing sun. He exhaled a puff of smoke and it slithered upwards into the sky, to perhaps merge with the clouds. She blankly stared at the smoke, at the clouds, and at the man. Then once again started walking towards him, her heart beating fiercely.

HER KNIVES

Of all the things she could have left, she left me her set of kitchen knives. The metal blades gleamed under my kitchen's fluorescent lights; the wooden handles lay flat against the kitchen counter. I found the paring knife to be cute, like the runt of the litter begging me not to get rid of it. Next to it was the Santoku knife, made in Japan, sharply arrogant on the counter, boasting of how it chopped, sliced, and diced anything she'd brought near it.

The knives were my mother's prized possessions and, every night after her day's work, she tended to them. My right hand was drawn to the rounded wooden handle of the chef's knife, my mother's favorite utilitarian blade. I held it up to my face, examining it, as if it somewhere hid a clue. It was a simple knife, no fancy manufacturer or exotic origin. The blade looked rather dull, and the wooden handle held a lingering smell. And old knife; I couldn't quite place the smell, so I brought it closer and sniffed, inhaling deeply. I examined it from all angles. The more I smelt, the stronger the scent became. I was becoming nauseous. It was not the smell of garlic or vegetables sliced long ago, nor indeed any type of food. It was the smell of … life. The smell of lives that had over the past decades disappeared down my gullet, choice cuts of beef and chicken, fillets of fish and pork rinds, the smell of unknown sacrifices that had prolonged my own life. The chef's knife seemed to look at me as if a warrior returning from a long battle to pay fealty to his king. It had silently been with our family through the years, keeping our bowls and bellies full, our hearts pumping, while its own hands were splattered in blood.

LOLA IN THE TILTED MIRROR

Under the snowflake speckled gray sky, the woman dreamed. She dreamed of struggle, wrestling with a mysterious figure in front of a mirror. A mirror showed no reflection of their tussle. The woman pulled her fists back and gazed into the mirror, her mouth ajar. As if it were a day's sky cloaking millions of stars beyond, the mirror reflected nothing. She was sure she was standing in front of the mirror alongside her opponent, yet the mirror was empty. She grasped at her own body and ran her fingers across her face, checking for the warmth of her flesh. In the distance, a voice echoed.

"Such a poor, despicable soul! Don't you see what's happening?" "Me?" The woman instinctively tensed her shoulders.

"Yes, you! Your wife, she left me a message before disappearing."

The woman raised her eyebrows, confused. Last time she checked, she had no wife and, unless she misremembered, would not have been interested. A wife?

"Pitiful! Wasting your time waiting for 'poetic inspiration' to strike. Meanwhile your wife works herself to the bone, alone. She doesn't deserve that. Nobody does!"

The woman stood, stunned at the insults. Was she a man or a woman? When did she become a poet, and worse, an indolent burden? The voice continued, giving her no chance to respond.

"Don't look so surprised. Sure, this place is tedious and dull. Perhaps the boredom drove your wife to despair. When everything you've dreamed comes true, that becomes the reality you seek to escape. Everybody needs an escape. Even you."

The more she listened, the less the woman understood. Images from a few moments before raced across her mind, her thoughts a jumbled, messy pile. Something poked at her core, prodding her pride and needling at her conscience. Perhaps she should go and find this so-called wife. She couldn't think of anything better to do.

"I beseech you, how can a lazy imbecile like me find this runaway wife? By which means do you suggest I search the multitudes to find the one?"

As she spoke, with each word her chest started to weigh more heavily, welling up with new information. Her wife's smiling face and the happy memories they shared began to surface and flash before her eyes. A tsunami of regret crashed over her, and brought her to her knees.

"Tsk tsk, to be at the mercy of your emotions is a weakness. Do not be fooled: that's just self-justification. You are not to regret but repent! You have hurt a woman, so now you will heal them all. You will help women achieve palpable beauty, something they can nurture and not only see but feel, too. Is this not a small price to pay to find your wife? Oh, and your wings. Of course, you'll need to hand them in as well."

"My wings? But … they're all I've got. Without them, I'm nothing."

The woman fought against the arms grabbing at her as she flapped fiercely. The spectacle resembled a pair of mating butterflies. Before she knew it, she felt an arm twist with blinding pain, the flesh of her wings torn. Blood-soaked feathers fluttered as she let out a scream, falling into the depths of an insensate darkness.

*

She woke from her dream, cheek pressed against a cold cement floor. She reached towards her shoulder socket. The soreness permeating each muscle suggested there would be bruising. The electrical current that prickled through each nerve reminded her what had happened. With a heavy groan she glanced over her surroundings.

She saw a clock. A clock reflected in a mirror, in what appeared to be a hair salon. The clock hands pointed towards nine. Her eyes followed the hour hand out the window. It was snowing.

She sat up, stretching as if she were the lead actress in the opening scenes of a play. She explored her stage on tiptoe, stretching her neck out like a goose. What a drab place. Out the corner of her eye, she caught a glimpse of her reflection and gasped out loud. She was fat! Her giant shovel hands seemed as if to belong to a man. Perhaps they could show benevolence. Her ample bosom perhaps carried a kind heart.

The clock chimed 9am, and the door of the hair salon swung

open. Brushing snowflakes off her black coat, a middle-aged woman scurried in. She switched on the lights, stepping back in surprise to find someone already there.

"Oh my! Oh dear, dear … let me see, you must be the new stylist starting today, right? The one from Galaxy Hair Salon, right? Good heavens, look at me, I completely forgot you were coming today."

She must own the place, the woman thought, and gave a shy nod towards the owner. The owner asked her name and, panicked, the woman released a garble of sounds. "Eh, oh, well, err …"

"What's that dear?"

The woman just nodded her head, waiting for this moment to pass. The owner scanned her up and down, clucking in disapproval.

"Lola, huh? Well … it's not the name I would have thought of, looking at you, but alrighty, sounds good to me! Hey, have we met before? I swear I recognize you from somewhere … I guess it'll come to me. Anyhow, it's a pleasure to have you here, Lola! I'm Madame Frieda Sheen, but you can just call me Freida. Welcome to Eden Salon!"

Freida shook Lola's hand, her fingers cold as icicles. Lola examined her new boss. Freida had a thin face, tanned skin. She didn't carry an ounce of fat, and she was short enough to perhaps be mistaken for a child. Yet there was something authoritative about her, and in the room she was a commanding presence.

The two women kept shaking hands enthusiastically, finding themselves at a loss for words. Underneath her big, blow-dried hair, Freida could not come up with a single thought. Lola could not muster a word to pass through her sleep thickened, dry lips.

Finally, Freida broke the growing silence.

"Welcome, welcome, dear. A helping hand is always welcome in Eden! Besides, business is booming during the holidays. By the way, how did you get in here? Oh right, I left a key with the receptionist at Galaxy Hair, right? Good heavens, I'm so forgetful today. The human memory is not to be trusted!"

Freida laughed at herself, tapping her temples. She pulled out a pink smock from the closet, then paused again.

"From your voice on the phone, I thought you'd be much more … petite, I guess.

Voices can be deceiving! Let's see … oh dear, what is going on with your eyebrows? I can barely see your eyes under all that fuzz! Come here, let me shape them."

Before Lola could object, she pulled a hair trimmer from the drawer, flicking the power switch on. Freida approached the bushy eyebrows like a sculptor with a mound of clay, and set to work with the buzzing trimmer.

"This job, I've got to be honest, you need to look good. Would you trust a skinny chef? We are beauticians, are we not? Oh, good heavens, how much hair do you have? And this, are you layering up for Winter? How are your legs so hairy? We're going to have to fix that."

Lola wanted to scream and run away. She bit her lip instead. Beauty was pain, after all. A part of her wanted to see for herself if the phrase held true.

The morning passed quickly. Customers trickled into the salon, one after another, sitting under machines with rotating, brightly lit saucers. The saucers dried hair, but reminded Lola of glowing halos. Another machine in the corner looked like an astronaut's helmet. Women would sit under the machine and close their eyes for an hour, as if calming themselves while taking a long journey. At the end of their journey, they would emerge with tightly sprung curls that defied gravity. This seemed a popular machine to sit below.

Snow started to pile up on the salon's windowsill, falling silently as if slowly erasing the colors of the city. Inside, women chattered loudly while TV infomercials buzzed through the room, like a warm light spreading from corner to corner. Lola had never touched another person's hair before, but found herself snipping away gleefully. It was as if she were under a spell.

Indeed, the salon had a powerful sorceress, and her name was Freida. As soon as her dainty fingers touched a customer's hair that person would, without hesitation, begin to divulge secrets. Real-estate tips from around the neighborhood were spilled, or a snippet of gossip about an illicit romance was whispered, or sometimes the dirty laundry of a family's secrets were aired. All Freida had to do was start attending to their hair.

Sitting under the saucers, one of the customers happened to be a singer at the local bar. Freida seemed to know her quite well. The singer entered the salon stiffly, her hands wrapped around her neck. Her vocal glands had shut down, and she couldn't even manage a squeak. Freida rolled up her sleeves, and began by washing the singer's hair, then blow- drying and intricately styling it. The singer emerged from her seat a glamorous diva, her voice booming across the salon. She had entered the salon a hoarse crocodile, yet left as a fluttering songbird. Hypnotized, Lola shouted 'bravo!' and clapped loudly as the singer left the salon.

Lola's standing ovation seemed to attract attention, and more women traipsed into the salon. Someone entered with untamed hair sprawling across her shoulders. "Do something, please, I'm about to go mad!" she shrieked as she threw herself into a vacant chair.

Freida approached her new customer with a smile, and her hands started to move hastily, like a head chef over a hotplate in the kitchen of a Michelin-starred restaurant. Her fingers danced, and while many entered feeling frayed and distraught, each customer left in a state of beatific calm. This particular woman, who turned out to be a lady of a manor, laughed gracefully while she chatted.

"You know that new soap opera, the one about the affair? Yes, the one everyone is watching. Well, turns out, my husband is having an affair with an extra from the show! What are the odds? I'm about to tear that bastard in half. Go heavy on the hair spray, I'm going to need this look to hold."

Freida agreed with the lady, letting out a surprised "good heavens!" or gasping "oh dear" every once in a while. She lifted the lady's spirits by clucking her tongue while whipping every last strand of hair into a perfectly crafted mound. The lady admired her reflection in the mirror.

Eden had a lot of mirrors. In fact, three of the four walls of this small, rectangular salon were covered in large mirrors. Each was carefully tilted at an angle to create a panoramic view for customers sitting in the chairs, so that Freida's work could be admired from front to back.

While she swept the floor, Lola glanced furtively at the lady's reflection. She stopped in her tracks, unable to take her eyes from the mirror. The lady sat in the chair in front of her, yet in the mirror's chair sat a different person. And it wasn't just a single different reflection either. Lola blinked and rubbed her eyes, taking a closer look at the lady in the mirror. Instead of a human face, she saw a face of a pig, a dog, a fox, and a snake, all laughing at her from different angles, as if she were looking into a kaleidoscope. It took Lola a few moments to bring her attention back to the real world. She checked

Freida's expression, to see whether she had any idea of what was happening in the mirrors. Freida chattered along with the lady, noticing nothing.

"Pardon me, ma'am, but were you born in the year of the dog?"

Lola asked. Then, before she could stop to consider if the question was appropriate, she blurted, "or perhaps the year of the pig?"

Freida looked at her, her left eyebrow raised.

"Have you recently seen any foxes? How do you feel about snakes?"

Questions continued to pour out Lola's mouth until the lady narrowed her eyes, ready to pounce. Freida stared daggers at Lola, silently urging her to shut up. Before Lola could explain, the lady cried, "how dare you! Ms. Sheen, you need to control your staff!"

But the lady's roaring was overshadowed; the door swung open, and a middle-aged woman entered, sporting a chic bob. Intellect and classiness radiated from her, perhaps befitting a professor. She glided into the salon, treading lightly across the floor, and sat herself down in a chair. Her roots needed a touch-up.

"Dark black for the professor, dark as ink!" Freida instructed. As Lola painted the graying roots, the professor pulled from her purse an egg sandwich. She nibbled, as if an alley cat sneaking over scraps. Potato chips completed her meal, crunching noises filling the silence with every mouthful. Crumbs fell at Lola's feet like tiny snowflakes. The professor did not care, she was too busy grabbing a packet of gum from her purse and popping two pieces into her mouth. She did not bother to offer anything to Lola, who did not particularly want the gum, even though her stomach angrily grumbled.   Grr. Grrrrrrrr.

Lola narrowed her eyes as she glimpsed the professor's reflection. Once again, the mirror was playing tricks. A Queen of Spades appeared, followed by an Ace of Diamonds then a Jack of Clubs. Playing cards shuffled and bounced around, yet the chair itself was empty. How strange. The professor seemed like she lived by the book, too strait-laced to be a gambler. Lola tried to search for a meaning within the cards, but failed to find a single pair. Perhaps it simply meant the professor's was a losing hand, that it was time to fold.

Lola looked away. What was the mirror was trying to tell her?

As the professor closed the door behind her, Freida and Lola sat down for a break. Realizing this would probably be her only chance to eat, Lola picked up the phone to place an order for lunch. Before she could dial, the door swung open. In came a pale young woman in her early twenties, with long shiny hair. She shifted nervously, asking whether they could shave her head. Freida clucked her tongue as she looked the young woman up and down.

"Oh dear, dear … we don't usually do that kind of thing here honey. There's a barbershop down the block. Or better still, I'm sure the Buddhist monks at the temple up the hill would do a spectacular job."

Lola decided to chime in.

"Very true, miss. Here we cut, perm, and style hair. We worship our customers like the good Lord himself, so we wouldn't know where to start with such a request. The monks, they're pros when it comes to what you're looking for.

Lola scrutinized the young woman. She couldn't be that old; at most, she was in college. Or perhaps she'd decided to skip college. Perhaps she was an activist of some sort, didn't militant types shave their heads in protest? The young woman seemed antsy. She couldn't keep her gaze fixed on anything and, behind thick-rimmed glasses, her eyes darted from corner to corner. Lola noticed that a lens in her glasses had chipped, as if it had been hit with a rock. Or perhaps a bullet! The young woman looked into the mirror, smirking at her reflection.

"Monks aren't the only ones shaving their heads these days. Plenty of celebrities on television have decided to go with the skinhead look. It's edgy, mysterious, even a little threatening. All this hair, it's too much. Letting go of it will be cathartic. I need to let go of it before I let go of anything else."

It was an unusual request but seemed to make sense. If the celebrities were doing it, they could do it as well, Freida said, grabbing the clippers. She examined the young woman's face. Perhaps she would have a cleaner, lighter look underneath this messy pile of hair. Freida took a deep breath, and boldly buzzed off half the young woman's hair. She then suddenly clutched at her stomach, apologizing to the young woman.

"So sorry, I can't hold it anymore. I'll be right back."

Freida ran downstairs to the bathroom. The young woman

stared blankly into the mirror, eyeing her half-shaved head. It was a provocative look. Lola looked down at the floor, at the pile of cut hair. She picked up a broom.

The young woman continued to stare at herself in the mirror through her broken glasses, expressionless and motionless. She then stood up from the chair, drawn to her reflection. She turned her face sideways, taking a closer look at the shaved side of her head, inching closer and closer towards the mirror. Suddenly, she jerked forwards as if she were about to bash her head against the mirror. Lola instinctively covered her eyes, wincing.

Before she could scream, the young woman plunged into the mirror as if jumping into a lake. All that was left behind were strands of hair, waiting to be swept away.

"Good heavens, sorry, that took much longer than it should."

Freida chuckled to herself as she returned. She looked at Lola, who stood paralyzed, and then looked at the chair.

"Wait, where did she go? And what's up with your face? Did she just up and leave? With … that hair? Without … paying? Good heavens, you have got to be kidding me. Ugh, I knew something was off with her."

Lola couldn't say a word. Even though she had just witnessed the strange event, she could not be sure if it had actually happened. What she was sure of was that nobody would believe her if she were to tell the story. So Lola decided to remain quiet. These mirrors had been playing tricks on her all day, but she wouldn't put up with it anymore. She looked away. But she could not stop herself from turning back, peeking into the mirror again.

Freida noticed.

"Oh dear, stop looking into the mirror so much. Your

reflection isn't going anywhere!"

Lola scratched the back of her head. She could beg to differ. Freida took a deep breath and smiled.

"It's okay dear, I know. Nobody is perfect, and it's difficult to love what we see in there. We all have flaws, at least everybody I know does."

Touched by her own words of empathy, Freida decided to continue to inspire her new protégé .

"We all still love looking in that damn mirror. Men, women, the old and the young, I have yet to see anybody who didn't care to look at their reflection, at least twice, before leaving the salon. Maybe they're trying to confirm something. Like, is that person in the mirror really me? The mirror is a true companion to humanity. I'd write that down if I were you, dear."

Freida was drunk on her own words. She continued to boast about how, as stylists, it was their duty and privilege to see both the beautiful and the grotesque within their customers, and guide each to find their own beauty.

Lola enthusiastically nodded her head in agreement. Fueled by her audience, Freida continued to speak on the history of Eden.

How splendid it was, especially during the holidays. Annually, at this time of year, the doors of the salon acted as a grand entrance to a majestic ball. Women would pour in, dressed in their finest furs and largest diamonds. Some would show off the latest work they'd had done, revealing newly bright eyes and plump cleavages. Women shared all sorts of surprising stories during the holidays, freely offering up tales of lust and desire, sparking small jealousies when comparing themselves to other women sitting in the next seats.

Roaring laughter would fill the salon until the end of each day, when they'd pick up their fancy garments and leave the salon, like actresses exiting a finale. After the glamorous events of the holidays, Eden would simmer down for a while, and fall quiet. Today reminded Frieda of one of those days.

"Hmm, I'm suddenly craving some hot, spicy soup. You want some?"

Freida nodded to herself as she picked up the phone, dialing the number of the local Chinese restaurant. As she ordered two bowls of soup, her eyes met Lola's. The two women smiled at each other in camaraderie.

"Ms. Sheen, are you married?"

Their quiet moment was ruined by Lola's random question. An awkward silence ensued, as Lola darted her eyes towards the frosty window. Snowflakes the size of fists fell outside. She heard Freida's voice slowly speaking behind her, deeper and quieter than before.

"Not anymore."

Anymore. Lola rolled the word over her tongue.

"He was ridiculously good looking, he made me laugh. Unfortunately for me, he was never the type to settle down. He left, on a cold snowy day like this, saying he had a job up north. I haven't heard from him since. Days like this make me wonder where he is …"

A dark shadow passed over Freida's eyes. She let out a sigh, her pointy nose twitching.

Knock-knock. The women looked up. That was awfully fast for lunch to be delivered, they thought. Standing at the door was not the Chinese delivery guy, but a woman, with bleached blonde hair that hung loose all the way to her waist.

"Are you here for a cut?" Lola asked.

The woman shook her head. Waves of gold danced left and right. "No, I'm not a customer."

Lola felt the hairs on the back of her neck stand. "I'm from Galaxy Hair … ?"

Sheen stood up, puzzled. Lola stood up, sheepish. Knock-knock. This time, the soup was here.

"Look, I'm going to need an explanation, but first, let's eat. I'm too hungry to think. Miss, yes you, have you eaten?"

The blonde shook her head, again, in the golden waves. Freida divided the two bowls of soup into three. Not a drop spilt. The three women huddled in a circle, and quietly slurped their soup. Once each pair of chopsticks had been put down, the three women looked at each other.

"So, tell me. Who are you? And who the hell are you?"

Freida pointed her index finger at the two standing before her. Nobody answered.

Freida leaned back in her chair, swiveling as she patted her stomach. The blonde scowled, baffled at the situation, and requested that Freida call Galaxy Hair to prove her innocence.

"Oh right, an easy solution, no need to dawdle here. Ask and thou shalt receive!"

Freida picked up the phone, keeping an eye on Lola while she dialed. The tension in the salon was thick as a ruff of uncombed hair. Lola and the blonde looked at opposite sides of the salon, Lola facing the window. The snow had thickened into a storm, the sky darkening to a darkly ominous shade of gray.

"Gosh darn it! The line is busy."

Freida shoved the phone into the pocket of her apron. She looked left and right, then came to a decision.

"Look, maybe both of you can stay. One of you can work as an assistant." Lola nodded happily. The blonde shook her head, snapping back.

"I'm an actual, legitimate hairstylist."

The blonde rummaged through her purse and pulled out a certificate. Lola took a step back towards the wall, trying to remember details from her dream.

While she stood trying to remember who she was, the newly arrived blonde stylist stormed out the salon. Lola didn't notice. She stared out the window, watching the snow fall, completely unaware that she was once again alone with Freida in the salon.

"Explain yourself. Who the hell are you? Why are you here?"

Lola stopped herself from blurting out the truth, that she had no idea. She knew that was not an answer Freida would want to hear.

"Tell me already, where are you from? The asylum in the woods? You seem like you've held scissors before."

Freida let out a long sigh.

"What a day, indeed. I spend the entire year looking for a decent hairstylist, and then in a single day two land in my shop! Sure, who could complain about receiving too many gifts from Santa … but for some reason, this feels different."

Lola looked into the mirror, and met the eyes of her own reflection. An image flashed in front of her, and she suddenly felt a spotlight shining down. The image grew clearer and sharper, as if she were twisting a kaleidoscope around.

"Oh, good lord!"

Lola shouted out loud. At least she thought she had; whether it was the volume of her voice or her rising excitement, her ears were ringing. Her heart raced like it belonged to a derby horse, and she shouted with delight.

"It was you! You were here this whole time!"

"Good heavens, you really are out of your mind. What in god's name are you talking about?"

"Please, please just listen to me!"

Lola felt a sudden urge to hold Freida, to embrace her tightly enough to never lose her again. Lola darted towards her, lips puckered, eyes ogling and burning with lust for

Freida, who instinctively backed away, hiding behind a chair. Lola started to chase her, the two women running in circles around the salon.

Chairs fell sideways, bottles rolled across the floor, expensive styling equipment crashed to the ground. Lola didn't notice … she was a beast blinded by desire. Freida was no match for her in height, weight, and youth, and when Lola caught up to her, she ripped off her apron and groped at Frieda roughly, ready to devour her long-lost mate as she pulled her closer. Freida snatched a broom off the floor, whacking Lola across the head. As Lola fell back, dizzily grasping her skull, Freida swung open the doors to Eden and ran out into the snow-filled streets.

*

Out on the streets, the darkening sky shed large cotton ball flakes of snow, as if the weather were trying to cleanse the streets and the people on it. Wiping the slate clean for new and as-yet-undefined dimensions to emerge.

With a closer look, perhaps one would be able to distinguish the snowflakes from the beings falling from the sky. Perhaps one would be able to discern the secret, that these beings were souls, maybe even angels. Some hanging upside down from snowflakes, some laughing hysterically and making hissing sounds inside the wind, and some merely stumbling downward through the air with tattered wings.

Underneath the snow, the two beings fervently ran, stopping to embrace then tear apart, repetitively, like children in an endless game. Running until they could no longer be seen, dissolving into the white and gray of the snowing night.

Ever since Freida and Lola were last seen in their dance of the butterflies, the salon's mirrors remain empty. Only objects reflect in the mirrors now, as if the salon is an uninhabited stage at the end of a play. Each mirror seems to wait patiently. Waiting for the owner to return and fill the room with light and warmth. Waiting for women to arrive with disheveled hair, shaking at their reflection, barely daring to recognize their own beauty.

Even today. The mirrors simply await.

AMUSEMENT PARK

The man was smearing shoe polish over a rock. The girl, my date for the night, yanked on my sleeve and asked, "is that strange? I could swear we just saw that guy!" Her front teeth bucked forward, and she twitched her nose like a bunny. Or perhaps it seemed so, on account of the set of rabbit ears she wore on her head.

"I doubt it."

I brushed it off, but still cast a second sidewards glance at the man. He was sweating profusely, arduously polishing the rock. Did he think it was a shoe? Was he out of his mind? The girl continued to insist that the man was the same guy who'd sold us tickets at the park entrance.

"Just look. Same hat, same shirt. Same guy!"

It wasn't difficult to have the same outfit. Employees of the park each wore the same uniform.

"It's just the outfit."

"I'm telling you, look at him! His forehead? That nose? The mouth?"

Perhaps. As I squinted to take a closer look, he looked at me and flashed a smile, stunning me on the spot. Perhaps she was right. This could be the same person that had handed us tickets at the entrance. Goosebumps formed at the thought.

Aware of our staring, the man kept looking back at us, as if he were checking to make sure he still had an audience. I pushed down on the brim of my baseball cap and reached for the sunglasses in my pocket. There was no need for sunglasses in an indoor park, but they seemed like a powerful asset when engaging in the art of gawking at the strange guy.

As I perched the sunglasses on my nose, the bright lights of the amusement park dimmed down and I entered a bubble, away from the noise and excitement. The world outside felt as if dimensions away, the girl as if a doll, and the park props that had momentarily amazed me seemed like simple toys.

"Hey, you Ray Charles?" The girl scoffed.

A wave of embarrassment washed over me, wiping out writings in the mind's sand. I pulled the sunglasses off, but couldn't decide if I should put them back in my pocket. As I fidgeted with the sunglasses, the girl adjusted her bunny ears. Meanwhile, the man had disappeared.

Ahead of us, at a wall, a group of children was bent over with laughter. The girl and I quickened our pace to see what the excitement was. We reached the laughing children to find a series of funhouse mirrors, bent and curved in all sorts of directions, distorting the reflection of those standing in front. One mirror would instantly dwarf the tallest man, while another would lengthen a young child as if they were standing on stilts. The slightest change in stance or angle would transform one's reflection completely. The children that had arrived before us howled with laughter as they posed in front of each mirror. After a while, they grew bored and moved to the next attraction.

When our turn arrived, the girl and I eagerly stood in front of a mirror. As we stepped forward, she shrunk to the size of a jellybean, while I was stretched like taffy. We switched places, switching fates. She soon towered above my tiny reflection like Gulliver on his travels, and burst into giggles. Empowered by her size, she boldly pressed her cheek against the curve of the mirror. The left side of her forehead bulged like a lumpy potato, and her eyes protruded, forming a gruesome creature. The same girl that checked her makeup with every reflection or couldn't bear the slightest wrinkle on her skirt, stood laughing at the monster in the mirror. I couldn't laugh with her. I did not believe in the world inside the mirrors, but they frightened me. I walked away before anybody could catch the rigid expression on my face.

The girl stayed longer. When she finally exited, her face was riddled with boredom.

She asked if I wanted ice-cream. Before I could answer, she ordered two waffle cones (chocolate, vanilla). I wasn't in the mood for ice-cream, but it was my first time at this amusement park and figured the girl knew better. Besides, it was the manly thing to do.

The ice-cream vendor handed over two cones with a wink. He looked familiar. I couldn't recall where I'd seen him.

The girl took her ice-cream and licked it proudly. I attempted to follow her example yet my tongue touched rock hard plastic. No, it felt like rubber. It looked the same as the girl's cone, but didn't come with the same sweetness, softness, or chocolate flavor I was promised. Dumbstruck, I held my display model rubber cone and stared as the girl licked her scoop of vanilla. She noticed me staring.

"What, you've never had ice-cream?" she sneered.

I decided to blame it on being lactose intolerant, and slyly tossed my cone in a bin. The cone hit the empty can with a thud. How did I end up with a display model cone, why me? I wanted to think it was a coincidence, the luck of the draw, but I couldn't help but think that this was something bigger. Somebody was messing with me. I didn't know why, but every fiber of my being told me something was amiss.

I looked down at my feet and up at the sky. The amusement park was covered by a dome ceiling, making sure this world stayed the same from daybreak to nightfall, Spring to Winter. The ceiling was interwoven with thousands of small square windows, each shut. The windows were merely decorative, and not able to be opened. Looking up at the ceiling, a sense of panic swept over me, and I realized this is what claustrophobia must be. I wondered what would happen if the power went out in the world under the dome, inside this glass bubble. I could picture the electrical rides shutting off and standing still, the once- bright alleys hushed and dark as a cemetery. The hairs on the back of my neck prickled with fear, but I cleared my throat and stood straight. I was with a girl after all.

"This place is lame. Shall we move on?"

The girl's eyes lit up, and she ran forward like a greyhound trying to win a derby. We weren't the only ones: a group of children ran next to us, one child leading the pack. Did they know where they were headed? I doubted it.

Amid the swarms of running children, we managed to push

ourselves onto the monorail. The girl was elated, chattering endlessly. I stared forward over the tracks, trying to locate our destination. The monorail wasn't headed anywhere, it just ran in circles. Once in a while it would stop at a red light and start again when the light turned green. It was an electric machine, but still filled the silence with recordings of train whistles and steam engine noises. There wasn't anything special about the monorail, it was monotonous as daily life outside. Yet the children found it exhilarating, shouting joyously and in unison.

The monorail liberated them, perhaps it made them feel limitless.

At the next red light, the girl and I stepped back onto the platform, and began to search for a new place to stimulate our senses or distract our minds. We scanned the map meticulously, finding the ship with a skull on its front.

There was a seemingly endless queue for the Pirate Ship. I couldn't help but look around; something in the air told me I should feel suspicious. There were no pirates of course, just a machine running the ship. It wasn't even a complex mechanism, and the ship simply shook up and down. I knew there would be no real pirate ship waiting for me, but the machine completely shattered the fantasy of being inside such a vessel. I looked around, searching for the person behind it all, the man in the dark conning everyone.

Children stepped onto the ship, waving their arms, and those who weren't shrieking were grinning toothily. As the pirate ship whooshed upwards, they threw their hands in the air. When the ship fell downwards, their smiles faded. With each upward rise, they smiled with a sense of victory; with each downward drop they scowled as if they had lost a game. The same machine repeating the pattern over and over again, and yet the children seemed to never see it coming, their reactions amplifying each time.

"Hey Mr. Serious, why the long face?"

The girl pouted as if I were ruining her fun. When I didn't reply, she pinched my cheek maliciously. It wasn't the pain that offended me; my pride had been hurt.

"Ouch! What is wrong with you? Do you not see that this is moving by a machine? Somebody is controlling the whole thing!"

I was surprised at the severity of my tone.

"Of course it is! What did you expect, real life pirates yelling ahoy matey?"

"You know nothing. The pirate ship is a lie. It's fake. Artificial. This whole park is being controlled by somebody."

I was insisting, yelling even, perhaps ranting.

"What I'm saying is, the joy in this park – this fake, artificial park – cannot be real.

It's a setup! We are just puppets in this controlled environment. That building? This cobbled brick road? The monorail, the pirate ship? Nothing is real in this park."

The girl stared at me.

"What has gotten into you? This is, no, you are so lame!"

She smacked me across the back of the head and walked away. I stood there, flabbergasted, the nape of my neck throbbing with pain. I reached out towards her, but she slipped past. Yards ahead now, she looked back and yelled.

"Nobody thinks this place is real. Believing it is real is what makes it fun! It's an amusement park, for god's sake!"

She headed towards the hot air balloons that promised to soar across the sky. They were plastic props that hung from rails, circling the dome. Children followed, running in the same direction. All it took was one child to start running to begin the stampedes. They didn't know better.

"Who do you think you are? Does it matter whether this is real or not? Doesn't it matter more that you actually enjoyed the experience?"

Her voice felt distant, light-years away. I stopped walking towards her and stood back in awe. She disappeared from sight. I had lost her to the crowds of running children.

A familiar face emerged from the crowd. It wasn't the girl. It was the man who had earlier been polishing the rock. I stared at him blankly. He had slung the rock over his shoulder as if it were light as a feather. He walked towards the park's exit, as if this play was over.

My body shook, a broken wind-up doll. The day's events flashed before my eyes, along with my doubts and questions. A part of my chest felt empty, and a sad, aching feeling permeated my bones.

Was it the girl, and how she'd disappeared? Or was it about what I chose to believe in, or rather, what I failed to believe? I looked around, getting my bearings as I repeatedly stroked my chest, comforting myself. That, at least, I knew was real. I looked up and down, at the extraordinary bubble that enclosed me, and tried to recall why I came to play here in the first place.

ABSTRACT ART FOR A SHERIFF

The local sheriff's office had been put on the case. It's always one of the three, the sheriff said: money, women, or power. The sheriff pushed up his black sunglasses. He always wore the darkest ones, regardless of the weather. It might not be that simple, the deputy retorted. The dead painter seemed to have had no interest in accumulating wealth, had a loyal wife, and was starting to build a name for himself.

The officers arrived at the house. They would begin at the core of the victim's circle, then widen their search to possible lovers and sponsors. Yet, before the lieutenant could ask any questions, the family broke down in unison, wailing for their loss. The painter's wife flooded the room with her tears, and the children were in their own flurries of panic. The lieutenant furrowed his brow, trying to find clues to piece together. Then the deputy butted in. New information: the painter hadn't died at home.

Red and blue lights flashed atop the car as they sped over the streets, the siren's noise shattering the city's peacefulness, accompanying both officers to the painter's atelier.

The paintings were simply a collection of abstract colors. At least that's what he could see. To the sheriff, the red was for a woman's lips, blue was the sky, and black reminded him of the night. Even he could paint this art, the sheriff muttered to himself.

He removed his sunglasses momentarily, and took a closer look. The painting was untitled. The deputy, who had been skimming through the painter's catalog, noticed other paintings were missing titles too. The few that had been named were 'Brown Above White', 'Lightness Above Darkness', or 'Red Above Black'. The sheriff shrugged it off. He directed his attention back to the main question: was the painter's death suicide, or murder? That was all that was asked of him from the folks above.

The sheriff rested his head against the untitled canvas, deep in thought. He couldn't figure it out. There were no people, no objects, or landscapes. All he could see were colors splotched on top of other colors. A Buddhist would say that it is not the appearance that binds you, it is the attachment to the appearance. Baudelaire would say that the most revolutionary occurrences happen under the roof of the skull in the fields of the brain. Yet the sheriff was neither a Buddhist nor a fan of the French Symbolist. He turned towards his deputy.

"What the hell is this … a joke? There's absolutely nothing here." "Sir, this is what they call 'abstract art'."

"Art my ass! None of this makes sense."

"Sir, they also say you see as much as you know."

"There has got to be some sort of explanation somewhere."

"Yes sir, there are some interpretations out there, but none warrant closer attention." The painter's atelier had an odd floor plan. The largest room was his main studio, with wall-to-wall windows and high ceilings. It was big as a small church. The floors were concrete, and boxes full of junk were strewn around the room. Canvases leaned against the wall, unorganized. As the sheriff flipped through some of these paintings, he noticed the last concealed a tiny door. He had to crouch to fit his body through.

The door led to a smaller, dusty, darker room. The windowless walls were painted dark brown, like the inside of a grave. A chill ran down the sheriff's spine. He felt as if he were wilting, and he was seized by a sudden urge to lay down. Something feels off in here, the deputy murmured as he reached for his gun. Definitely, the sheriff agreed, as he reached for his chest. The stench of the paint felt as if it had seeped into his organs, and made him nauseous.

They rushed to find an exit, hurrying forward through the next door they found.

This led to a different room. How many hidden rooms did this place have?

This room, coffin-sized, had space only for a small daybed, with a dingy old quilt spread over the top. There was something small hanging at the headboard. This must have been the room where the painter ate and slept. A pang went through the sheriff's chest.

How sad. Leaving a good house and loving family behind, cooped up alone in this hole … and for what? Paintings that made no sense. The sheriff shook his head. He must've been mad. The world could be divided into two types of people: the evil and the insane. Those were the people that paid for the sheriff's livelihood, so he figured he was no different from them. He felt the same pity for himself.

He realized that this narrow, small room had been painted a dark red, like the inside of one of the heart's chambers. Like the inside of a mother's womb, an ancient tomb, or a clay jug that once held a precious liquor. It was palpably not a large room, but it felt like it was at the core of something. Once again, the sheriff turned towards his deputy.

"You tell me, what was this guy trying to paint?" "Sir, perhaps he painted reality as he saw it." "Must've been mad to think of reality in colors." "Seems like it, sir. To each his own, sir."

"All right, all right, you can stop lecturing me now."

He waved the deputy off as he examined more closely the item hanging on the headboard, squinting. He tilted his head, changing the angle, and stepped back, trying to look at it as a part of its surroundings. He did not see any particular color. All he saw was dust lingering in the room.

The deputy had excused himself to go to the bathroom. Either he must have ate something bad for lunch or was taking a smoke break. Whatever the reason, he was taking too long.

Left alone, the sheriff retraced his steps back out to the first room, the main studio. Outside, it was now dark. The sheriff switched on the lights. Rows and rows of light bulbs lit up the studio. Light bounced off the windows' glass, transforming them into mirrors reflecting a room full of light. In these mirrors, the light rays seemed to continue infinitely, until one could not tell where the inside of room ended, and the outside of the world began. The sheriff stood, blankly staring. What was this? All he could see was light and dark.

Something told the sheriff he had to take another look at the paintings. His feet led him back to the row of canvases, where he now stood, in front of the nearest painting.

The canvas was divided in half, black above gray. He took a step closer, looking for answers. The closer he got to the painting, the more he felt like he had traveled into space. Perhaps it was because he'd heard it was dark in space, he wasn't sure, but that was how he felt. He nodded. At that very moment, the untouched canvas fell backward. It was never a canvas, it was a door, leading to another room. The sheriff's eyes widened.

The room behind the canvas was a bathroom. The sheriff awkwardly cleared his throat. This was definitely the painter's personal private space, he muttered, feeling like an intruder. The walls were covered in mirrors, even the back of the door. And the ceilings. The sheriff felt surrounded, with no place to hide.

His hand instinctively reached out for the mirrored wall, searching for some sense of assurance. Everywhere he touched, an endless array of terrified men stood waiting. The men followed his every faltering step, every movement. The men were almost gruesome, their faces pale with trepidation, hand after hand gripping at their guns. There was no enemy in sight, yet the men in the mirror had the eyes of rabid beasts waiting to attack.

Further down the line they merged together into a beast swallowing heads whole, fusing shoulders, linking arms like a chain. Petrified, yet wild and savage. Like the line of men in the mirror, the sheriff's head had also started to spin out of control. A chill ran up and down his spine, and beads of sweat formed at his forehead. He couldn't stand it anymore. What was it? What did it mean? He pulled the trigger.

ONE CLICK

All it took was one click for the order to complete. At the tip of my finger! While listening to the 9 o'clock news! What else could this finger do? I wondered, grinning at the screen. A single click could summon to my doorstep a golden statue of Buddha from the exotic depths of Asia. I could build a Fortune-500 company from the ground up, or hire a thousand servants to clean my room. A click could bring me true love, while another could kill my worst enemies. What a time to live in: the era of the Click!

Typhoon Bolaven was on its way, the weatherman announced on the news, with a somber, stern tone that was sure to cause the country's alarmists to shake in their boots. The only thing shaking in this room was the finger adding items to my cart. Bolaven baloney, who cared?

I checked the items in my cart: a leather hat, leather boots, leather gloves, and (drum roll) a leather jacket. Final clearance sale. Satisfaction guaranteed. Free shipping.

Everything was made of genuine cow leather and, even better, with this month's paycheck I could afford it. When you made as little money as I did, you could not ignore the words 'Final Clearance Sale'.

"Oh brother, I didn't know you were pursuing a career as a ranch hand. That would be the only explanation for all that leather in this day and age," my sister mocked, looking over my shoulder.

"Hey, leather is making a comeback, missy. Looks like somebody needs a little less Cosmopolitan, a little more Vogue," I scoffed back with my nose aloft.

She rolled her eyes and groaned. "You probably want to check when that Vogue was issued weirdo, it's almost 90 degrees outside."

"Oh, I know what I'm doing," I boasted, "it's called 'off-season'. It's Econ 101, sister, supply and demand! You buy ahead, when nobody realizes that they want it yet. It's called an investment, ya' hear?"

Speechless, she stuck out her tongue and disappeared from the room.

The news anchors were still discussing Typhoon Bolaven, their voices booming across the living room where my parents were spending their evening, as usual. The volume was at full blast, but it didn't bother Dad. Laying on the couch, he went back and forth aimlessly between picking at his ear and then his nose. Mom was sitting on the floor amid the morning's sprawled newspaper. Atop of the morning headlines lay a massive pile of garlic that she was peeling. Her eyes were glued onto the screen, while she sniffled every now and then.

"If you've ever heard of the Butterfly Effect," the weatherman spoke, "well this is how the winds begin. Somewhere far, far away, probably along the equator, a small movement happens. It starts out something minuscule, something nobody would notice, but it travels across the ocean, above the isles, through the jungles and on top of the mountains, collecting its power. Before you know it, it has gathered into a giant typhoon. This Typhoon Bolaven of ours looks like it started along the west of the north Pacific, and we are seeing some insane numbers when it comes to wind speeds. I wouldn't be too afraid though, after all, the wind is …"

Achoo! Achoo! Aa Aa ACHOO!

The weatherman's rambunctious chuckle was suddenly overshadowed by the sound of Mom sneezing. Mom usually had a soft, almost mosquito-like voice, but when she sneezed it was thunderous as a lion's roar. The dramatic sneeze that caught our attention was soon followed by quiet muttering.

"Surely this one sounds like drama. Way too much drama for ordinary folk like us. We'll be fine, right?"

"Of course, dear, of course. Back in the day, I've seen typhoons bigger than this. Back then we didn't have these sturdy buildings, just our flimsy old houses, and we still survived without a scratch. Seoul is an impenetrable city. We'll be fine."

As Dad reminisced, Mom sat by his side, enthusiastically sneezing.

That's when the 'Purchase Complete' page appeared on my screen. A confirmation text alert dinged from my phone simultaneously. 'Your payment has been received! Thank you!'

A week passed; each night accompanied by one strange dream after another. In my dreams I went from being a caveman hunting wild beasts with a single spear, to lassoing cattle as a cowboy in the wild West. I slaughtered buffalo as the chief of a native American tribe, for my people that believed I was half man, half beast. I became C3PO from Star Wars, declaring myself half-human, half-machine, roving across galaxies far, far away. With each dream I believed, no, knew that this was the one and only reality. I would wake up in a frenzy, hanging upside down from bed sometimes, my bedsheets crumpled and sweaty. It was as if I had discovered the secret to time travel; my bed was the portal.

Within that week, packages started to arrive. Even though I had ordered everything together, each item was delivered separately, from different vendors. The leather gloves arrived first. Made in China. At a quick glance, the quality of the leather seemed decent. Yet when I flipped them over, I found that the palms were knitted with wool. I opened my next package to find my leather hat, also from China. My order was for dark brown. This was more burgundy than brown. I shut my eyes while opening the third package, hoping my boots would be amazing enough to make me forget about the first two. Unbelievable! This had to be a cruel joke. What I found was a bastard of a shoe, somewhere in between a sneaker and a fisherman's boot, with botched leather festooning the side.

I felt like I was having an aneurysm. No, a heart attack. Vertigo! It felt like all my bodily circulations had halted, my skull cold and lacking blood and oxygen, while my skin burned. So this was how people dropped dead from anger.

When I finally received the box with the leather jacket the next day, fear set in. I debated simply not opening it, but that didn't last long as man is merely a slave to his curiosity. I held the jacket up against the light. It reminded me of a clown's costume, patches of different leather pieces sewn together to make ends meet for this sad excuse of a jacket. This was the last straw.

Huffing and puffing, I dialed the customer service number. Whoever was on the other end of line was going to get an earful. My sister poked her head into the room, then ducked out without a word. I begrudgingly listened to the monotonous tone of the automated voice, dialing one digit after another, then smashing zero over and over again to 'Speak to a Representative'.

I demanded the stammering customer service rep connect me to the top of the chain. They were about to lose one very loyal customer and, on top of that, I could tweet up a storm about the whole experience. Hell hath no fury like a customer scorned! The Korean customer service rep insisted that the customer is king, and that they were trying as best they could to resolve my problems. Except they couldn't solve anything, as the online shopping company was headquartered in the US. They gave me the number for the customer hotline there.

"He-llo! He-llo! I, uh, have a plob-lem."

My thick Korean accent didn't throw the American customer service representative.

In a calm and collected voice, the man asked me repeatedly if I had read the terms and services of their website. Of course I hadn't, nobody reads those things, you just clicked 'I agree' at the end. The man continued, saying that they were merely a platform, the middleman, and that the actual manufacturer was responsible for the product quality. The manufacturer number I was given was a +86 number. I groaned loudly. China.

"Ni hao, ni hao! Wo you ... wèntí! Wo you gè wèntí"

I pulled every word I remembered from my high school Mandarin classes, talking to the Chinese subcontractor company on the outskirts of Shenzhen. The Chinese man on the other end spoke as if we were in a fight, his tongue sharp as a sword. Clink, clink, clang clang! He continued to pour words towards me left and right, loud and fast. Slowly yet surely, with my elementary command of Mandarin I continued to get my message across. In the end, my Korean perseverance must have won him over, as he reluctantly gave me the contact information for another company. According to him, he too was a mere middleman, simply a manufacturer following instructions. If I had a problem with the product, I should go to the designer. I looked up the company name, opening a fresh email draft. This email was going to Grenoble, in France.

"Bonjour, Je suis Coréen. J'ai été un clientde plaints ..."

The French replied to my wordy email within a day. I guffawed at their reply: the French blamed Brazilian grass! Grass! Essentially, the problem was in the material itself, not their fabulous, flawless French design. They attached the initial design sample in the email, which looked exactly like the picture on the shopping site that had initially piqued my interest. They were very sorry for my inconvenience, but there was a problem with the grass that fed the Brazilian cows that were used for the leather. They hoped I could understand. Also, if I had any further questions, they would reply after they returned to the office from their summer holiday.

Clack c-c-clack. I clenched my jaw, gritting my teeth as I flipped through the pages of my old geography textbook, landing on the pages that showed the world map. With my clicker finger, I traced the route that my leathered goods had traveled. It was all that I could do at this point. The whole world was involved, seamlessly connected, yet nobody was to be held responsible!

That night Typhoon Bolaven hit, heavily, a brutal force rolling into the metropolitan city and over the sturdy building in which we lived. I woke in the middle of the night to the sound of my window shattering, and hurried to the living room, to find the windows there unscathed. The next morning, I learned that our entire building had survived the night without a scratch. Except for my place, Unit 404, in my bedroom only.

It didn't matter if the city was impenetrable, or how far modern man has come in his brilliance. Nothing, simply nothing, could beat the wind.

What Lies Under The Blood Moon

Shush! They'll hear us.

Why, why should we be the ones shutting up?

They can't know the secret. They can never know of the secret! You mean they don't know it yet?

They don't. And it will stay that way! How tragic.

That night, the clouds in the sky nibbled the moon as if it were a loaf of bread. A monkey and dog, chained at the door, greeted us as we entered the restaurant. A taxidermist's eagle, shark, and leopard hung from the walls, proudly staring us down as we took a seat at our table.

I wondered why a fine dining restaurant in the middle of Seoul had chosen taxidermy as their main theme. Perhaps it was a ploy to lure wild-hearted guests. Or perhaps the owner was a hunting enthusiast. Regardless, it was a popular spot, and the chosen venue of the night to celebrate my boss's recent promotion. We had a rather large group for dinner, and my boss had invited a cluster of important and semi-important employees from departments across the company. Each invitee had some lengthy achievement to brag on and on about. If you were stuck on the listening end, you had to smile and nod along, struggling to feign interest.

Cigarette smoke and chatter filled the air. The smell of grilled meat soon followed. I stuffed my mouth with beef and sipped wine until the night filled with an array of moons and my limbs struggled, entangled in a web. Words were spoken, though at this point I was unclear whether they came from my lips or someone else's.

Just look at those guys. What? Who?

The omnivores over there! The ones chomping on bloody flesh, drinking bloody red wine, laughing like fools and flashing their teeth.

Ah, the humans.

Oh well, we can never know whether they're human or not from the outside, can we? But let's call them that for now. By the way, did you hear? Our captor is moving on soon.

Where to?

Tsk tsk, use your head. Where could he possibly go? Anyway, what do you think will happen once he disappears? Things won't change around here. You think either one of us will end up on the wall?

What an odd conversation, I thought. Looking left and right, I tried to find the source. People laughed, drank, and joked with one another across the table. It was impossible to distinguish one voice from another.

The guy next to me belched out loud. Before I could say the words 'how rude', he farted. The combined smell was too real for this to be a hallucination. I lifted my head, away from the clouds of bodily gas, high enough to locate the truth behind the voices. The creatures sitting by the door. It couldn't be. Or could it? Was I hearing their words? Or was I simply hearing things?

Fools, utter fools! You little chained-up things?

I sprang out of my seat like a chased gazelle. My head snapped towards the new voice.

Dust fell slowly from the tip of the eagle's wing, like pixie dust. The voice continued.

Look. Who in their right mind would go through the gruesome effort of stuffing you, preserving you for eternity? Do you have magnificent wings like mine? Spots like the leopard? Are you at least as cute as the blowfish when you get angry? Look at yourselves: mutts like you line the streets, and common monkeys hang from trees. Hence, I ask you, who? What could possibly be in it for them?

The monkey and dog stammered at this wrench that had unexpectedly been thrown into their debate. I too staggered along with them, uneasy at the sudden intervention. It seemed natural considering that I had the worst seat at the table, at the end by the walkway, closest to the door. I heard them up close, like they were whispering in my ear.

Tsk, tsk. Monkey, kiddo, stop feeling sorry for yourself. It's pathetic. You could've become, evolved into, whatever you want to call it, a human a long time ago. Now look at you, all tied up for nothing. And you, my canine fellow! Wagging your sad little tail up in the air when you're actually pissed off. What a sight.

I leered at my surroundings, trying not to be conspicuous. The monkey's face was as red as his butt and the dog whimpered, pawing at the floor. I felt stuck just looking at them, it was almost suffocating. I loosened my tie, tilting my head left and right, wriggling my neck to try and take in more air.

Hey, pay attention and take a look at yourself!

I was convinced the sarcastic voice belonged to the eagle. The moving beak confirmed it. Could it be? I looked at my boss. He was entirely focused tonight on drinking and chattering. I briefly debated talking back to the eagle, in defense of the monkey. As my lips were about to part, the sound of chains clinking stopped me. The monkey, eyes red with fury, was ready for a fight. He looked straight ahead, then around to each side. He fiddled with the chain around his neck, then started to speak with a trembling voice.

Now see here eagle, enough with the chains. You see that guy at the end of the white table, drinking his blood-red wine? You see what he has around his neck, made of silk? That my friend, is a decorative chain. And he's not the only one! That entire group over there, the one that works on the 70th floor, every one of them has a blue lanyard hanging around their neck. Like a cat collar with bells. It's a necessity for those of us who have to work for a living, you see?

The dog decided to speak up too, encouraged by his friend. A-a-and you're no better than us! Dead and stuffed.

Ha, dumb as a dog, indeed. What's the point of being alive when you have no freedom?

I have no pain, no conflict, no chains. Nothing holds me down.

Now, now, dear eagle. You can't deny that at the end of the day, we're all just slaves to our owner. But who knows? Things could change with a new owner.

Absolute morons. I told you earlier, fools, no freedom, no life.

You sit there wagging your tail when you are actually ready to bite somebody's head off. You're a sycophant, a coward. Can you deny it?

The eagle continued to chastise the two addressees. His words were sharp as his beak, incessantly snapping at the monkey and dog, who both shriveled back. Silence briefly ensued.

The clouds had completely swallowed the moon at this point. Yet the moonless sky refused to go completely dark. From afar, stars sparkled like a scattering of white sugar. There was more to the sky than just the moon. I looked across the table. It was true that I too, had wanted a promotion. After all, I'd spent my best years slaving away from the bottom rungs of the company's ladder. It would be nice to have an office on the top floor. Yet, perhaps that wasn't the only way to shine. As long as I lived and breathed.

Ahem. The eagle cleared his throat, breaking the silence. He proceeded to talk in a softer, more sympathetic tone.

Kids, let me tell you a story. I heard it from the leopard, my friend on the wall over there. It's a real tear-jerker you know. I heard it, and I swore to myself that I would never live like a slave. Never. Over my dead body. You guys ever hear about the elephant with the huge ears, the one who could fly, Dumbo? There's a whole movie about him, yeah? Apparently, Dumbo was modeled after a real elephant, an African elephant named Jumbo. See, Jumbo lost his mother to a hunter. Orphaned, he was captured and shipped to the London Zoo. He was an instant star of the zoo, when the big guy stomped around, it was like London Bridge was falling down. In the beginning they caged him up, didn't really show him to the public. But then, somebody came up with the idea to have an interactive exhibit for the kids, and they made a whole show where for two pence, you could feed him biscuits or treats, and Jumbo would grab the cookie right out of your hand! People loved him, loved that big guy! The star of the zoo, Jumbo would perform during the day, but then would act odd, even delirious, at night, doing stuff like rubbing his tusks against the floor. Probably traumatized, the poor guy. As a teenager, he started to become aggressive. The zoo tried to control him, smacking him with leather whips and hooks with nails in them, but nothing seemed to work. At the end of their wits, the zoo sold Jumbo to an American circus troupe for ten thousand pounds. So, Jumbo crossed the Pacific. The circus trainers were much worse than the zookeepers. They started soaking Jumbo's bread and biscuits in whiskey. They were boozing him up to have him move, feeding him four liters of whiskey a day. In a year, Jumbo fell ill, and none of the humans could figure out why. The ringmaster knew that Jumbo would still be a huge attraction after dying and made plans to stuff him when he died. It was around that time, on their way back from Canada after a show, that Jumbo tried to cross a set of train tracks. Bam! Got hit by a train, dead on impact. As soon as Jumbo died, the ringmaster called his taxidermy guy, and the guy got to work. 'Dead Jumbo' became a permanent show at the circus, following the circus everywhere it went, moving the audience to tears every time. The audience loved him; kids revered him, and with the movie, he's loved forever.

Ugh, humans are the worst! How cruel!

The monkey cried in agony, his eyes bloodshot. The dog howled at the moon like a lonely wolf.

I mean, why are we fighting each other? We're just victims, all prey.

Rightly so! We can't blame each other for our extinction. We should blame … him.

That guy.

The monkey started shrieking, jumping around maniacally, while the dog bared his teeth and snarled, his claws clattering on the floor. They looked straight at me. The eagle also glared at me with his piercing black eyes from the other side of the room.

Me? What, why? Why me?

Shocked, I stood up from my seat, my finger pointed at my chest. The drunks at my table grabbed at my sleeve, urging me to just sit back down. When did he get so wasted, they muttered, fingers wagging in front of judgmental eyes. Don't go and ruin the mood, they jeered. None of that bothered me. I was a man on a mission, and I was going to stand my ground.

What did I do wrong? I'm just a nobody, I couldn't hurt a fly! It's you, your kind!

The eagle, monkey, and dog came at me full force, screaming at the top of their lungs. How unfair! I'm a victim as well! It's not my fault. It's … theirs!

Shush! A hushing noise cut through the night. It echoed across the room and out into the dark.

Now speak up, say it to my face! Anybody, this is your chance. You are the ones responsible for this mess, no? You got anything to say for yourselves? This, this is the real barnyard, the real animal farm.

I pointed in anger towards the aggressor. It was then that I realized my finger pointed towards nobody, just empty space. Perhaps they'd hidden under their chairs, trembling with fear. Or perhaps they had already left, calling it a night. Either way, my colleagues were no longer there, at the end of my fingertip. I rubbed my eyes, wondering. I slapped at my cheeks, suspicious. I saw nothing, I heard no one. There was no us. There was no them. All that remained were the beads of sweat trickling at my temples. This had to be a nightmare.

My Upstairs Neighbor

Like clockwork. Her nails tapped against my window. Once, twice, three times. I scurried out of bed, leaving crumpled bedsheets behind. I rushed to the door in silence before the others woke up. It was nice to be distracted from my sleepless night spent tossing and turning. She stood in the doorway, wearing a sheer white nightgown. Barefoot. Unbrushed hair loosely hanging down her back. A portrait I had been haunted by.

She couldn't sleep. At least, that's what she said, pushing her palm towards me.

Kettle corn. I smirked and opened my hand. Kernels of kettle corn dropped into my palm one by one. A few didn't make it, dropping to the floor. Oops, my bad! I looked up as I apologized in a flat tone, checking her expression. Her face was ghostly pale. There were tangles in her hair, which was split at the ends. Buttons barely hung onto the threads of her disheveled nightgown.

"Can't have coffee in the afternoon anymore, huh?" I shrugged.

"Or are you restless from an uneventful day … ?"

Silence. I pulled on her sleeve, leading her to the stairs by the fire exit. Moonlight spilled in through the tiny glass window, painting the staircase silver. The stairs creaked under our feet. I thought I caught a glimpse of her smiling. For no reason. There was no reason to smile in the middle of the night.

She lived by herself, free to do what she pleased. And she really lived it up. She was unpredictable, spontaneous. She spoke hysterically, unapologetic and loud, cramming in as many words into a single breath. Once she got through her story of the night, she would calm down and poofff, disappear back upstairs. Like cigarette smoke into thin air. She was like that.

I didn't know much about her. For starters, I had no clue what she did for a living.

She didn't seem to have a regular schedule; she didn't leave her place upstairs during regular hours. She didn't have visitors either. Every month or so she would dress up for some fancy occasion, complete with lacy skirts and dark eyeliner. The scent of her perfume would linger. Other than that, she rarely left the house. She seemed to have a lover that she liked to complain about. Their relationship was complicated. I had never seen him in the building. He came and left like a stray cat in the dark.

"He smashed my window today …"

My heartbeat elevated at her words. She didn't notice. She never noticed. She shoved her wrists out towards me. Bruises, black and blue. The size of quarters. It wasn't easy sitting there, listening to her complain night after night. It wasn't difficult to feel pity for her, though.

Why don't you do something about it? So passive, so quiet.

Speak up, we live in different times now. Why, if it were me … I stopped myself from blurting out. She didn't notice. She never noticed.

"Talk about throwing a tantrum, kicking and screaming. Hurting himself."

Some men just couldn't control their temper. He was probably drunk. Men were like that sometimes. He probably wouldn't remember in the morning. I guess that's just what men often do.

"He took a razor blade …"

"He what?" I shrieked out loud, unable to stop myself. "But at the end of the day, we still love each other."

It was pathetic. She was pathetic. Domestic violence hotlines and family resources would be no use. She was blind with love. She was a cliché from a bad movie about a bad relationship.

Through the tiny glass window, the moon slowly inched westward. What day was it, I thought to myself, then remembered that tomorrow was the anniversary of my father's death. There would be a dinner. I needed to go grocery shopping in the morning. There would be a lengthy to-do list. As dawn approached and tomorrow slowly became today, I twitched with angst while listening to her repeat once more her pathetic story.

My lips trembled.

Why should I listen to you? At this hour? Night after night.

I wanted to yell. Shake her even. But I couldn't. I hesitated. The words stayed in my mouth like chewing gum that had long lost its flavor. Perhaps she noticed. Perhaps she noticed this time.

She blurted out of the blue, "I'm an unhappy person."

"Unhappy?"

"Yeah. I'm unhappy. And lonely."

"Well, isn't that a choice for you? Please … just … please."

It was the first time I had spoken to her like this. Silence ensued. "You'll regret that."

"Why? Please, I can't do this anymore."

The sound of my heartbeat loudly in my eardrums. It was all I could hear. She had nothing to say anyway. She was like that. Like that, when you thought she would be like this. Here, when you thought she'd be there. She lived alone, but then it seemed like she didn't. She spoke like a crazy person, but then as eloquently as a speechwriter. She was a victim. Or was she?

As the moon slowly faded, the woman's face grew even more pale. We stood quietly, looking at each other's half-lit faces. She kept her silence. I kept mine. She looked at my face, with a blank expression. As if she were trying to read my thoughts.

"It's not just about me."

Blood rushed to my face, spreading like ink dropped into a glass of water. Every inch of my body burned, as if an ant under a microscope in the sun. I mean … what … who do you think you are? My tongue quivered, like a warrior ready to attack. I fumbled to find my words. The warrior soon lost morale.

The morning winds picked up, rattling the window, which was slightly ajar. I stood quickly to close it. Through the tiny glass window, day was breaking, fracturing the dim night. I turned back towards the stairs, now painted a dark shade of gray. I found kernels of kettle corn, sprinkled across the shadowy stairs like stars strewn across the sky. One, two, three kernels on the steps. Kettle corn that we'd shared. My upstairs neighbor and I.

MISS CHAMBERS AND HER PARROT

Her eyes opened to his chipper greeting. Purrrty, so purty. He repeated it twice. Miss Chambers slowly sat up from her bed and headed towards the bathroom. She peed and showered, still half asleep. Then she opened the closet door, grabbed a work-appropriate two-piece, and stood in front of the mirror. She reached for her hairbrush. Purrrty, so purty! He squawked with vigor.

She told him to shut up, but truth be told, she didn't mind. She kept an eye on him reflected in the mirror while she applied toner. And lotion. And some extra cream. She patted her face down before the moisture could escape her skin, which seemed especially dry from yesterday's nightmares. He approved of her decisions. Purrrty, so purty.

Ignoring his words, Miss Chambers gripped a dark pencil and closed her left eye. Eyeliner required detail and focus. Her hand slipped at his next outburst. "Purrrty! So, so purrrrrrty!" She poked her eye. The pain left a wet, dark smudge.

"Gosh darn it!" She shrieked out loud. "You ruined everything!"

Miss Chambers scowled, tightening her lips until she could feel frown lines begin to form. Feelings of guilt soon followed. He was just being nice, she told herself. She sheepishly looked back at him.

He wasn't her first. He was a gift from a missionary that had just returned from Africa. The missionary told her the parrot's name was 'African'. She thought about giving him a new name, but nothing really seemed good enough. So, for now, she simply referred to the parrot as 'Him'.

'He' was different, at least compared to Padma Sambhava, whom she had lived with before. 'He' was more sensitive, more eloquent. He greeted her each morning, and he bid her good night. He was more in-tune with her feelings, and he knew when to pay the right compliment.

As was usually the case, he was the one to yet again reach out for a truce. Hello, hello, he apologized. She returned to the reality of her morning routine, glancing at the clock. She would need to hurry. She chose a bright shade of red for her lips. Purrrty! She must have made the right choice.

He was so different from Padma Sambhava. Samba was a naysayer, constantly searching for her faults. Samba rambled nonsense throughout the day and nagged at her until she felt like pulling her hair out. "Turn it off!" Samba would yell when she sat in front of the TV too long. "Not good, not good," Samba would mumble when she sang to herself. Padma Sambhava reminded her of her father. The tone, the words, and the way Samba repeated everything three or four times. A spitting image. Things this time were different. 'His' words warmed her like hot chocolate, and she couldn't imagine life without his candy-coated compliments.

But then again, he wasn't as good looking as Padma Sambhava. Most people couldn't differentiate one parrot face from the other, but she could. They looked as different as night and day. The only thing they had in common was that they mimicked the words of humans, but that was just part of their nature.

Every girl in the office wanted to look pretty, it wasn't just Miss Chambers. Looking in the mirror and telling yourself you looked pretty was one thing; feeling pretty was on a whole new level. 'Pretty' held no meaning until somebody else agreed. She thought about how God had created such beauty in nature, from the shining sea to the sparkling stars.

Why couldn't such generosity be extended to everyone? Miss Chambers questioned this lack of consistency.

She let her train of thought run freely, carefully applying the finishing touches to her makeup. She checked her labor in the mirror. She wondered if she looked pretty. Perhaps she didn't. Then she shook her head. Old habits die hard.

Beside her, the phone vibrated. As she reached out, she felt a gust of wind come from the phone. She must be losing her mind, she thought as she answered. The voice on the other side asked, "is this, Ms. Verda Chambers?"

For a split second, she froze. She often forgot that she even had a name. "This is … she?"

Her stomach tightened with the answer. As she listened, the knot in her stomach burned like a fireball, ready to explode. Apparently, she had left her number at a raffle for a cosmetics company event. She didn't think much about it, she never won anything. Yet this time, it seemed, she had. They had chosen her name. The company employee on the line thanked her for being such a loyal customer, and offered his congratulations.

A trip to Europe. For fourteen days, no less. She resisted the urge to break into a dance, but that did not stop her from clapping loudly. Her heartbeat joined the applause. She lifted both arms in the air and yelled, hooray! She spun around, laughing until her ribs began to ache. She spun again, then stopped, as her eyes met the cold stares from the grey bars of the birdcage.

Well, shit. She wondered who could take care of him. Nobody came to mind. He was too talkative, too noisy, too annoying. He was messy, he needed constant care. Every three days or so he would need to be taken out of the cage for new bedding, fresh water, and more food. He wasn't the easiest companion.

Miss Chambers hunkered down with her phone. She called the office to take a personal day, something she had never done before. She called her friend, the one that had married first and already had two kids. The friend answered, then hastily hung up saying that her youngest was allergic to birds. As a last resort, Miss Chambers called her sister. Her sister sighed, warming up for the marathon of nagging that would soon follow. How Miss Chambers was becoming the crazy bird lady, and how she would forget what it was like to be loved, to be touched, by a man. Miss Chambers hung up. Her phone lay in her limp hand. She pictured the lights of Paris, the streets of Berlin. She could hear the music of Vienna and the chattering crowds of Rome. She was not ready to let go, not just yet.

She detested asking people for things. It made her feel pathetic, the hassle was too much. Yet the desire to go on this trip was stronger. Her eyes darted left and right, glancing past the mirror, then fixing on the reflection. Her face was too round. Her body was passable, but her face was round as a pancake, almost a perfect circle. She had been born in the wrong era. In the old days, her full cheeks would have been a sign of affluence, to be desired and revered. Nobody wanted that now. Like many other women born with outdated features, she too had thought about plastic surgery, but she was scared of both the process and the price.

Something hit a nerve, with a piercingly sharp pang. She thought about the girls in TV commercials. The twinkling eyes and frail frames that graced covers of magazines. The perfect jawlines, perfect teeth, and the annoyingly perfect smiles.

She, too, had once been on a quest to love her true self. For a long time actually, it's not like she hadn't tried. She wanted to change, yet she didn't know how. All she knew was that she had a strong desire to pack up her life and go somewhere. Perhaps she could be somebody else, somebody new, in a new place with new people. It was possible. A part of her knew that, and that belief had burned a small hole in the corner of her mind. The more she thought about it, this trip was not just dumb luck. It was an answer to her questions, her doubts, and her prayers.

She started dialing, once again. She went down the list of contacts, reaching out to those she was close to, and to those she wasn't. Nobody said yes. By the time she put down the phone, the clock suggested it was time to call it a day. She leered at the cage, at her ball and chain. He looked straight back. Purrrty, so purty, he mocked with vigor.

Those words she heard all day, every day. It felt strange how the same words had such different meaning now. She stared at him, scanning every feather. He flapped his wings in the air, cooing the words purrty, so purty. The words from his hooked beak whistled through the air, echoing from corner to corner, and attached themselves to her. Entering an ear, the words traversed the labyrinth of her brain, free-falling through her skull, landing in her mouth, flapping around her tongue like a fish out of water. She could taste the salt, feeling a wave of seasickness. She felt something prickly coming up her throat, as if spider legs were crawling up across cobwebs from places she'd kept screwed down tight since long ago. She could feel them pry their way out of her tightly sealed lips.

"Lies, all lies," she screamed, over and over. She could hear herself and her tone, but she could not stop. She could no longer ignore it, brush it away. She could no longer forgive, not anymore. Her hand busted through the cage door. Her fingers wrapped tightly around the parrot's body. It was hot. And squishy. Purrrty, so purty.

An Unfamiliar Place

I turn my head from one side to another, carefully scanning my world as if with the eyes of a newborn. Snowflakes flutter through the window in front of me, gliding like feathers in the wind. I blink slowly; once, then a second time. And then I gaze towards the revolving doors on my left. Two women enter through the shimmering portals. Am I seeing double? The women look alike, from the tops of their neatly combed dark-haired heads, down to their black trench coats and leather pumps. Two birds of a feather.

I push the thick glasses back up the bridge of my nose to get a clearer view. The pair glides down the marble floor of the lobby, flawlessly aligned, like soldiers marching to a drumbeat. Backs straight, toes pointed, heels clicking in perfect sync. My eyes trail after them until they exit behind another set of doors, and I shake my head. Does such a thing as a four-legged human exist? A sudden voice interrupts my thoughts.

"What the hell is this? Who are you? Who are you, and who the hell am I? You tell me, 'cause I got no idea, no idea at all!"

The demanding tone is more than enough to draw my attention. An old hag sits in a wheelchair, knuckles white from gripping the handles. She complains, in a croaky voice, to another woman. Probably her daughter. The old hag repeatedly asks, no, demands that she say who she is. Her words echo through the lobby.

You could play tennis in this lobby. I look across the vast open space, up at the high ceilings, and back at the revolving door to the side. Everybody in this lobby has someplace to go. They hold precious things in their hands. They carry heavy things on their backs. They hang onto things, other people. They push themselves forward with their arms, and with their wheels. They all scurry through, across the lobby towards their destinations. I look at the shiny marble floor. It looks slippery. Yet nobody seems to fall.

I sit and stare at the busy crowd, like a bystander, an anomaly, a foreigner. A man in a white coat brushes past me, knocking the coffee cup from my hands. The man dashes across the lobby, chased by another man. The chased man holds a knife in his hands. The chasing man shouts for help, as he limps behind his target. "Catch that man, somebody, catch that doctor!" He, too, wears a white coat. The lobby buzzes with anticipation, as the crowds momentarily pause to find out what happens next. Two bulky security guards in uniform stomp in, grab both men, and drag them from the lobby. Perhaps they were both patients? I can only assume. In the calm after the storm, the crowd thins as people turn back towards their destinations. As if nothing happened in the first place.

As people exit one door, others enter through another, without skipping a beat. I look past the bustling crowds, and out the window. In the deepening snow, snowflakes crash down aimlessly, painting the chaotic portrait white and grey. Have I been transported to a faraway land? I shake my head vigorously, as if it were a magic eight-ball with an answer.

A woman in a wheelchair passes by. She holds up a frail arm, which is connected to an IV drip. She nonchalantly throws a piece of trash on the ground. Another woman walks behind her, swiftly cleaning up. The woman in the wheelchair continues forward, creating a temporary trail of litter behind her. The second woman follows, silently picking up the pieces of gum wrapper and used tissues, patiently gathering them until she finds a trash can. I can't see either of their faces, as both are concealed by long permed hair and flu masks. I find the duo's endless cycle of littering and retrieving litter somewhat amusing, somewhat sadistic, and somewhat masochistic. I wonder if they have some sort of agreement. Do they know each other? Was this all part of an act?

Although … who would do that? I muse to myself as I look around. Snowflakes as large as my fist crash against the window. The café in the corner infuses the air with aromas of fresh bread and coffee. The ATM machine whirs with delight as it counts and dispenses thick wads of dollar bills.

The revolving doors whirl around. An expecting mother waddles in, her round belly cradled in her arms. At the same time, a new mother hurries out, her crying newborn held tightly in her arms.

That was fast! Or was it? The world, my world, starts to spin like the revolving doors. I hold onto my seat. Perhaps my brain is broken. Perhaps the revolving doors are magic. Who knows at this point? I pull off my smudged, foggy glasses. I hear a child whining.

"Again? Nuh-uh, no! I don't wanna! Not anymore!"

The whining is interrupted by a loud sneeze. An old man, clutching onto his cane, corpse-like, sneezes so intensely that his brittle legs shake from the aftershock. The young boy is taken aback, and quiets immediately. Sure, it was a misunderstanding, but at least it works on the kid.

The momentary silence is soon filled again with whispers and chuckles. The old hag in the wheelchair, the one that needed to know who she was with earlier, walks hand-in-hand with the younger woman she was with earlier. The two women giggle, as if they share a secret, walking towards the exit. I look back at the window. Snowflakes jag down like flying daggers. I'm no longer sure if it's snowing or raining. I stare out the window.

Ah yes, I must be at the theatre. Yet, it is unclear whether I'm part of the audience or part of the cast.

I rub my eyes like a child waking from a nap. I rub my temples like an old man with a migraine. I slowly make my way to my seat, to where I'm supposed to be. At the front desk, the hospital staff work with vigor, frantically typing and talking. Double-digit numbers flash on screens above, ringing loudly each time a new number appears in place of an old one. I go sit quietly in the corner.

The nurse calls out numbers, calling people one by one to the desk. Her hairstyle reminds me of flight attendants. She loudly announces the next number: 44! Nobody responds. She looks down at her chart, brows furrowed. She looks up and calls the number again, waiting for movement from somewhere in the crowd.

I look at the paper slip in my hand, the slip that has the same number written on it. Should I stand up? Or should I pretend not to notice? I hesitate. I hear the clock ticking. I see the nurse pouting.

She continues to call out the number. She calls out a name. I slouch into my seat, crumpling the paper slip in my hands. I don't recognize the name she's calling. Is it my name? I'm not sure. Her tone goes up a notch, and her colleagues gather around her. The nurses hush, discussing something. Their murmuring intensifies.

I shut one eye and keep the other open, until it starts tremoring from the pressure. Then I close them both, deciding that this is the best excuse for not responding. The noises prevent me from keeping up the act. I take a peek, my eyelids slightly ajar. The scene continues, as if I had pressed pause for a second, then resumed. Same scene, same people, same act.

I blink. I sit there blinking, in the middle of the bustling lobby filled with sickness, like an old man trying to remember his youth, his purpose. Why am I here? What's going on in this act?

It is a riddle, an enigma. An unsolvable puzzle. I turn my head, looking out the window.

Snowflakes glide down aimlessly, the size of palms ready to slap me across the face. I stare at them, waiting for something, someone. The icy winds of the north blow forth a new batch of snowflakes, and one particular snowflake catches my eye. The snowflake, as far as the stars of outer space, viciously flies towards me. Whoosh! It shoves itself through the corner of my unknowing eye with a stinging sensation, melting into my reality.

LIES, ALL LIES

In Memoriam: Baik Nam Jun

I used to be a stray cat. One of those cats that you see lurking through the alleys in the dark, eyes shining in moonlight. That kind of stray cat. The kind of cat whose coat has never been brushed, whose nails have never been clipped, whose soul hasn't been silenced. My idea of a fancy feast was a night out by the dumpsters of Manhattan's fine dining scene. My idea of a treat was discovering a dropped chunk of tuna from some Wall Street guy's salad. You know what kind of cat I'm talking about. You've seen me before. You've seen hundreds of me in this big city, everywhere you look.

We're not all the same though. Unlike the many others you may look down on out there, I'm cultured … hey, I listen to opera. And jazz. And I have dreams. Vivid ones.

What does a cat dream of, you ask. I dream of those ancient times when I was a big cat from the gods. When I was a holy creature. I was the messenger of the gods, with my glistening coat of gold, a thunderous roar, and eyes drunk with power. Every now and then I still hear myself roar, somewhere deep inside. When I haven't eaten for a while. When I haven't met a lady cat in a while. Moments of desperation make me think back on that roar. But I digress. After all, I'm just a mere kitty cat, who once served a master.

Where do I start. When we said hello? Or when we said goodbye? Anything and everything that has a beginning also comes with an end. Master was the one who taught me that. About impermanence. I guess if I were to ask him, he would say that it wouldn't matter. He said he didn't live linearly, that he wasn't bound to rules. The ultimate free spirit. Others called him a nomad, a man beyond borders. Some said he was a mysterious wizard, creating concoctions between the East and West. Some worshiped him as the king of Avant-garde, blurring the lines between art and technique. Some called him a fanatic, a fraud, a fiend. Everybody had an opinion on him. He didn't give a damn. He just lived his truth.

My master passed away on the last day of the lunar year. On the day the sun clapped its hands together saying, 'that's a wrap!' to the year. On the night when the sky swallowed the moon whole. Along with the moon, he disappeared. Master always had a fondness for the moon. He followed it, loved it, worshiped it, and destroyed it. When the moon was full, he worked through the nights with vigor, and when the moon waned, he lay wan and helpless, without inspiration.

People misunderstood him. They laughed when he spoke sincerely, when he wasn't joking at all. He would continue, regardless, stammering in a foreign language, trying to get his point across to the rooms of scoffing people. Sure, now they call him a genius. They idolize him now. Like all great artists, he was before his time. He was arrested once. He was often mistaken as a homeless person. When he unveiled a new piece to the world, people mocked him, calling him crazy, his work a piece of junk. Just look at us now. Look at the TV screens, flashing throughout this jungle of a city, holding us captive day after day.

Turns out he was a prophet, holding up a mirror to our generation.

He adored the moon, the Earth's lover, but his passion stemmed from Pluto. It was like he relied on Pluto, as if he received signals from it. There was a destructiveness inherent in my Master. Like the goddess Kali with a sword in one hand and a skull in the other, he held his hammer high, smashing convention and monotony. Elegant violins folded in half, beautiful bow hairs slashed. Coloring in the lines was out of the question. Boundaries shouldn't exist in art in the first place.

People jeered. Look at the lunatic going at it again. Nevertheless, the image would stick with them. He would make people think about things again. "Lies, all lies!" Master said. According to him, art was just a sham. I'm still not sure how much of that is true. After all, I'm just a kitty cat. Such a statement takes courage, though. And I can't believe that anyone would muster such bravery simply to tell a lie.

I guess I've never told this story. It was one of those weeks: my weeks of misery, pity, and hopelessness. Out of despairing starvation, I gulped down the first thing I could find. Unfortunately for me, that happened to be a poisoned rat. As I rolled around in pain, clutching what seemed to be the last of my nine lives, I saw a shadow approach.

He stopped in his tracks, observing the hopeless creature before him. He hung me upside down and beat me with a bamboo stick. I closed my eyes, thinking that this was my death. I woke up shaking, and soon, following him. Of course, he didn't want a cat. I had no intentions of having a master either. Yet, it was too late. Destiny already had her ropes winding tightly around us.

He would look deeply into my eyes and lament. "You, too, must be a tiger. You hear it. You dream it. It must be." My spirit was trapped in a miniature version of itself, not my fault, but because of man and his civilizations. He told me to live up to the tiger I was, commanding me to eat, sleep, breathe, and dream like one. I would sheepishly lay my head at his feet, unsure what he meant. I watched Master intently while he voraciously ate, or relaxed loudly, or growled while sleeping. I yearned to learn from the best, from the man who was the most formidable of tigers.

Every morning Master woke from his slumber, bright-eyed and startled, as if he were the first one witnessing the first day ever. How strange, how surprising, to be gifted with a brand new day. He would stride onto the streets of New York, with the prowess of a tiger, ready to amaze the world. How did I know all this? Because after our first meeting I spent every living moment with him. Because I heard every word that escaped his lips, even the ones that were not intended to be heard by others. Perhaps his words to other humans weren't always the truth. After all, he didn't trust mankind.

*

On the night of Master's passing, the stray cats of New York came out of their alleys to weep and wail. To this day, cats still roam the moonlight thinking of him, missing and remembering him. Did your city, Seoul, feel the same? Did you also miss him? Master imprinted on the cats of New York a lasting legacy. He taught us to hold our heads up with pride, that we were the most dignified of beasts. Our lives were to be playful and light-hearted, and the world was our forest to roam. We may pick at scraps, but we would feast like kings of the wild. As long as we ignited the memories of when we were tigers.

I am not saying tigers are invincible. Undeniably, tigers have weaknesses. Not to mention being penniless. Man no longer fears the ferocious beast. Oh, the savagery, the barbaric persecution! Now, great tigers only roam behind bars. Oh, how the mighty fall! This crushing tragedy paralyzes me, weighing me down as if my paws have been trapped in cement and my body has been tossed into the Hudson. Honestly, it feels so overbearing that some days I wonder if this life is worth living. Yet we animals don't quite have the means to take our own lives. And so I continue to carry on, day after day. At least this way I get to see my master's work finally recognized. I get to see my master's spirit recognized. Finally.

He was a wanderer. A lunatic moon. The Amur tiger. A true artist. My master. But ultimately I will always remember him as a free man. I still wonder why he loved the moon with such fervor. And yet, when I look up at the sky, I find myself smiling, drawn towards the peculiar magic. Perhaps Master lives on the moon now. I hear his voice calling when it's full. I see his crooked smile when it wanes. My wondrous one, my master of the moon.

The Visitor

On the first night of the Dragon year, I dreamed of my mother. She visited my dreams again the next day, and then again. Seven nights in a row!

Upon arrival on that very first night, she told me she needed to pee. She hurried to hike up her skirt and squat down, urinating an endless stream that flowed like the Mississippi river. It started off glistening gold, then eventually turned milky white towards the end. A part of me knew I should have turned my eyes away, yet they remained glued in awe to the strange sight. She finally grinned with relief.

"Good lord, I've been too busy to take a piss, can you believe it?"

She spoke with vigor, much like how she would when she was alive. As was usually the case in my dreams, I was a young girl. Mother was back in her forties, maybe early fifties, much younger than she was on her deathbed.

"Listen, could you move me from the temple to a better one?"

It was her first request.

"Why, you don't like it there? They're supposed to be the best for Buddhist funerals."

I could hear my squeaking voice and the tone of resentment within it. Mother always had some kind of request or complaint towards me when she was alive. Arguing back had become second nature to me.

"Right, you're right. There's no doubt about it. It's just that I don't feel that comfortable anymore."

It had been ages since we'd seen each other, but we still couldn't look each other in the eye. Perhaps it was nerves. Perhaps it was the guilt.

I had taken a risk, or rather, a leap of faith keeping Mother's ashes in the Buddhist temple. Not only had my mother and I been baptized in the church, but my in-laws were devout Christians too. I attended Christian schools, and there was even a time in my life when I was referred to as a Born-Again Christian.

Mother was barely a Christian, but she liked to say 'Good lord', a lot. The Lord must have listened in on her prayers, because we somehow ended up in America. We planted our roots as immigrants and relocated our family tree. Just like Mother wanted.

When Mother died, we had an American funeral. We got to say our awkward goodbyes to an open casket, as Mother lay there in her favorite outfit, face fully made-up, positioned like she had simply fallen asleep. After the cremation, and countless heated conversations with my sisters, we decided to divide Mother's ashes into three. A third of it went to Los Angles with my younger sister. Another third went to New York where my other sister worked. The rest came with me to Korea. As if we were dividing a loaf of "holy" bread. It seemed ironic to make this kind of equitable division in a matter that was strictly spiritual, but we had grown up in America, living and breathing democracy.

And yet night after night I tossed and turned, unsure of what to do with my third of the ashes, wondering how I could make it up to Mother. That was when a friend told me about the Buddhist temple. The temple would hold a traditional Buddhist funeral for the deceased, and the monks would pray daily at dawn to ensure the spirit was at rest. I may have only had a third of Mother's ashes, but her entire soul could rest in peace at the temple. I made my decision, and along with it decided not to share the news with my sisters.

The matter was put to rest, and so were my sleepless nights. Or so I thought. Mother continued on in a hurried voice, as if she were running out of time.

"It wasn't so bad, even sort of fun in the beginning. It was new, different, almost comfortable. I would hang out at the altar, above my number, above my name. Don't look so surprised, it's not that bad. Everybody does it. When you don't have a physical body to be bound to, you're no longer bound to physical spaces either. You're light. You're free. Like air. Like music. Like sunlight! Right before the sun rises at dawn, before the sky shifts from pitch black to dyed light blue, I would hear the wooden drums. That means a new day has begun. And alongside the drums starts the chanting of the monks, their prayers. I hadn't realized how beautiful it was, not when I was alive. The monks chanting is almost as soothing as the hymns at church. So why do I want you to move me? When it's so peaceful out there? Well, you listen to me girl. People don't change. Even when you're dead, you don't change. You know how everybody dies? How death doesn't discriminate? Yet, some things don't change, even when you're dead and just a spirit without a body."

Before I could tell her that I had no idea what she was talking about, she stopped me and whispered in my ear, "I'm only telling you, and I'm only telling you once, so listen carefully." She placed a tiny red book full of incomprehensible illustrations in front of me. I followed the tip of her finger through the pages, confused by the squiggly drawings, illegible codes, and sketches of unrecognizable animal features. Yet I nodded along faithfully, as if I understood everything.

I woke up from that first dream in a frenzy. I tried to remember what she said, and what the illustrations meant. I couldn't remember her words, or what I had understood to begin with. The more I tried to remember, the hazier the memories became.

Luckily, Mother visited the next day as well. She droned on like my old college professor, repeating, explaining, emphasizing, and summarizing her words.

"So … long story short, I want to leave this place. It's not that I'm not happy. If you want to move me to a different Buddhist temple, fine, I could get used to it. It's just that …"

"What, what is it Mom? I can't wrap my head around this …"

On the second night, I looked my mother straight in the eye and asked her to her face. I was even younger than the girl I was the previous night. Mother looked at me with warmth, whispering softly. She hadn't changed at all from when she was alive, not one bit. Her expressions, her tone, her gestures, and her thoughts were all those of the Mother I once knew.

"I'm telling you, you'd think death would be life-changing, but nope! Doesn't change a thing in old folks. There's this new lady on the altar, a stubborn old cow I'd say. She is the absolute worst!"

"What's so horrible about her?"

"Horrible I say, good lord! The old hag was an overzealous follower her whole life, lived well beyond her years, and dropped dead with nobody to shed a tear for her. Sad, right? I was trying to be all nice and empathetic about it, but ugh, she hates my guts. For no good reason! I mean, I'm not the most likable person, I suppose. But this woman just glares at me all day, pouting, glowering. Here I am, just trying to get along with everybody, and she starts telling me off. How dare I rest there, taking up precious space on the altar, when I'm a Christian. There were a bunch of other souls there too, and not all of them are Buddhists, I swear. But this lady doesn't care. She just ragged on me in front of everyone as if I had committed treason! I'm telling you … it's really starting to get on my nerves."

"Seriously?"

"Dead serious. I swear on my own damn grave. Why would I lie to my own daughter?"

"Pfft, Mom, I know you're telling the truth, I'm just saying, who cares about that stuff after dying? I can't believe this old lady. So, what did you say?"

"I tried to explain. Given the circumstances, I was exceptionally calm. How Christians don't believe in reincarnation and how my daughter wanted my soul to be taken care of. I'm not sure if she was jealous, but she didn't even pretend to hear me. She just kept ranting about how I didn't belong. How I had no sense of loyalty to my religion. She really put me in a corner!"

"How petty of her."

"Extremely petty! I put up a good fight though, showed her who's right. What's the point of fighting over religion at this point? There are no borders or passports in the afterlife. She has her own principles though, I'll give her that. She kept saying there's a difference in karma. How she had earned her spot, but I took the shortcut by letting my kids pay for mine. She laughed in my face. I tried to ignore it, but those words cut deep."

"Unbelievable. Why does that matter to dead folks?"

"Well kid, believe me, it matters. Nothing changes when you die. Death doesn't suddenly transform petty assholes into holy saints. This might sound like I'm lecturing you, but listen carefully. The only time you can change, people can change, is while you're alive. Not in the afterlife. Anyway, the old cow really stirred things up at the temple. The spirits started to whisper, and this led to a roaring debate. There are three major parties: devout Buddhists, parents of devout Buddhists, and the rest of us. I'm a bit of a rarity, since my children and I are all Christian. Plus, I've lived abroad. I get it, I'm special."

Her eyes twinkled with arrogance. I wanted to call her out on it, but decided to hold back.

"People really don't change I see."

Mother was obsessed with academic prestige. It was why we had college degrees despite growing up as poor immigrants. She still held on to her fixation in the afterlife. I briefly wondered whether there were alumni groups in heaven. I shook my head at how ridiculous it was, feeling a twinge of anger towards our academic infatuation. Even inside the dream, I could feel my heart start to palpitate and my blood begin to boil.

"Good lord, calm down, will you? I'm just telling you how

it is, no need to overreact. Jeez. I'm just here because I'm uncomfortable. My life down here wasn't all smooth sailing, and I'd like to be at peace now. You get that, right? You're my daughter, you should know. Just move me somewhere quiet, where there aren't any mean spirits. Maybe that temple in the middle of Central district. Or the Elite Temple, I hear that place is quite prestigious.

Somewhere classy. Oh, well, it may not matter. As long as they pray for the spirits every day. Heck, I'll take whatever you choose for me. I trust your choice. But you get what I mean, right?"

For the next five nights, my mother and I bickered about the same matters, like we would when she was alive. She had come to me before the situation got worse, before the spiritual debate became a religious war. She came to me to plea for comfort, to help put her soul to rest. I couldn't say no, and I started to make the arrangements.

Perhaps it was the new year putting me in a new mindset. Perhaps it was that she talked about it for seven days until I got it. Perhaps it was that I simply got what she meant; I was her daughter after all.

Night Picture Of Rain Sound

Adam Cloud closed the book slowly, murmuring the final sentence of the novel. He traced the spine of the book with his fingers, then tenderly caressed the hardcover. He inhaled, deeply, his beating heart beginning to calm. Reading was his comfort, his escape; an ultimate companion. He dreamed of becoming an author one day. One day, he would write such a novel himself. He leaned back on his futon and looked out the window.

Raindrops tapped against the window glass. It wasn't rainy season, yet it had rained for the entire month. An entire month of gloom, doom, dampness, and wetness. He hadn't been to work in a while. What was the point? His was the only mouth to feed in this house, after all.

Knock-knock. A visitor? Startled, Adam looked at the clock. It was too late for anybody to visit his humble studio. Too late for family members to visit from his faraway hometown. Too late for friends from the city to swing by. Too late for a girlfriend to come over. Ha! He wished he had a girlfriend.

Thump-thump-thump. Whoever was out there was pounding the door now, louder than before.

Could it be the rain? Too loud, and too sporadic to be raindrops. He grumbled as he got up, then poked his head out the door, just enough to stay dry, and looked up at his uninvited visitor.

Adam could not believe what he saw.

It was her, standing between the slanted sheets of rain. She had the same clothes, the same bag, the same face. At least it was the same face that Adam had imagined. There she stood, in the streaking rain, as if conjured.

Yet, how. How was it possible? The woman had just courageously left her home, leaving everything behind. She lived by the sea, and always carried the scent of the waves with her. At least she did in the novel, he mumbled to himself.

As Adam stood there dumbfounded, the woman pulled out a wad of papers. It was a lease, signed and dated. She insisted that she was supposed to live at the studio starting this month. The month that started this very day!

"But I live here."

Adam said the words out loud, but felt his voice shrink with each syllable as he flipped through his memories. Memories of his landlord's dull face. Memories of the old- man musk in the air whenever he dropped by. Memories of his landlord's monotonous voice. He tried to remember his last conversation with the landlord. It wasn't pleasant.

"Oh no, did you not receive notice?"

The woman frowned, lines creasing her forehead.

"Look, I've had a long day. I'm just tired from all the travel.

Would you mind if I came inside for a bit, out of this rain?"

Where were his manners. Adam reprimanded himself. He sheepishly moved aside, realizing the poor woman with the suitcase had been standing in the rain the whole time. She hurried in, shivering from the cold. Drops of water fell from her clothes to the ground, each glistening like a fish scale. Some of the drops stayed atop her head, shining as if tiny seeds between the locks of hair.

As she stepped into the room, his tiny studio seemed to balloon, like adding yeast to make bread rise. Feeling faint, Adam sat down and pinched his own cheek. It hurt.

The woman was just as he had imagined. Her round face. Her round, shiny eyes that reminded one of small buttons. Her mouth, pursed with determination. At least she looked like the woman he had sketched in his head. Yet there were some details that he hadn't imagined. Like how she carried the stench of sweat, reminding him of a day laborer. He couldn't help but be disappointed. She was supposed to smell like waves. He pinched his nostrils.

On the other side of the room, the woman was starting to take offense. Sure, she was a nobody from the countryside, but this wasn't fair. It took her a long time to save up the money to get here. God only knows how much patience and endurance it took. She wanted to call somebody who could come to help her sort out this situation. She fidgeted with her phone, wondering who that person would be.

Nobody came to mind. Absolutely nobody. Annoyed and stumped, the woman looked back at the doorway she had just walked through. It was still raining, and the clock on the wall suggested that the streets downtown would be empty, dark, and unwelcoming.

After taking a minute to stare blankly, the woman pursed her lips and sprang up, starting to tidy the studio. She gathered the books that were strewn across the floor, prized opened the one window to let in the rain-soaked air, and unfolded her handkerchief so as to start wiping layers of dust from the corners.

"Excuse me. This is still my studio. At least until today, that is."

Adam protested, but his voice did not come out as loudly as he thought it might. He found his tone surprisingly wheedling.

"Not anymore!"

The women spoke assertively.

"Don't you dare touch those books! I have a system. Just hold it, will you? It's not like you're a genie from a lamp, or a shoemaker's elf, or one of those fictional …"

At that point, Adam stopped himself. He could be right, but he could also be wrong, and he didn't want to be called a crazy person. Not again.

The woman did indeed look like the character from his novel, but she certainly didn't seem to act like her. She was obnoxious, unrefined, and demonstrated a 'see if I care' attitude. The heroine of his novel was quiet, gentle, somber, accommodating, even heart-wrenching. Who was this woman?

How uncharacteristic of her. A perversion of the character's core, the ultimate plot twist. Off the pages of his book, she was a whole new being with her own free will. Can such a change be possible? He eyed the cover of the book laying on his futon. Was he insane enough to imagine such a thing? Where was the line between reality and fantasy? Had there ever been a line to begin with? Adam thought about pinching his cheek again but decided to give his head a vigorous shake instead.

"Miss, umm no, Ma'am, you're crossing a line here. At least 'till today, legally speaking, this is still my studio. If you must do something, do it tomorrow."

He remembered that she was older, at least that's what he assumed since her character in the novel was married. Her marriage was her cage, and she was supposed to be a free bird that had just burst out the cage. He scanned her up and down, disappointed now at what he saw.

"Legally speaking? You want to talk legalities? I am the person rightfully entitled to live here, and you, legally speaking, should be out of here. Out in the rain! Out in the middle of the night! Legally speaking, my ass! Let's see about that!"

She rummaged through her bag and pulled out her phone as if it were a weapon, scrolling through her contacts. She tapped on the landlord's number. They stood in silence as the phone rang. Once, twice, no answer. She didn't know who else to call. He didn't know where else to go. Outside, it was dark as the inside of a wolf's mouth. The wind howled, as the rain pattered against the window. He felt a wave of anger break over him.

"Ma'am, maybe Missy, whoever you are, barging in on me in the middle of the night? This is an intrusion."

"An intrusion?"

"Yes, an intrusion! This is clearly an invasion of my rightful home."

"Look, I have rights. A legal right to be here."

Adam glared at the woman until he felt pressure in his temples. This wasn't the woman he'd read. Perhaps he was wrong this whole time. It seemed she was somebody else. Perhaps … but then again. It was like he had fallen into a vortex, where time-warped and there were no continuities between places, or people, or events.

"Look kid, just look! Look around. There is not a single place to sit down in this junkyard you call home. Every inch is covered with books. This might be hard for you to understand, but I'm a little claustrophobic. I can't stand small, enclosed, chaotic places. I can't tell you why, but I have my reasons."

Adam looked around. His little studio didn't seem chaotic, exactly, but it was small. Feeling a pang of guilt, he tried creating space for her. He took a big step back, just big enough to accidentally trip over the pile of books she'd just moved. As his head hit the floor, memories from the novel flashed before him. What was her name? Mooney … Looney … Luna something? As far as he could remember, just before he passed out, that woman was claustrophobic too.

The novel that Adam had just finished started off with a woman named Luna, a victim of domestic abuse, and the story ended with her escaping her old life. Her husband had been a penniless bar singer, a drunk, and a rogue. Yet he had a beautiful voice. Luna loved him, totally. He loved her too, in his own way. Adding to her misery, she falls pregnant. She hopes that this will change things, that this might change him.

Nothing changed. The abuse continues and, in the end, she escapes it all, venturing into the world in search of a new life.

"I'm just so tired, so exhausted. I need a place to rest …"

Her words pulled at his heartstrings. He sneaked a look at her waist. Her face was pale, and her frail limbs were too bony. Yet her belly seemed round and full. She must have felt his gaze, and she turned around, resting her hands on her back.

"I've been through a lot, believe it or not. I'll spare you the details, it's not like a kid like you would understand anyway."

"No, I get it. I read about it all."

Adam spoke with a soft voice, perhaps for the first time that night. The woman from the novel was around thirty, so she was much older than he. He wanted to formally introduce himself, to tell her he was turning twenty tomorrow, to ask her name. A part of him thought it was too much, that it could be an intrusion. And so he swallowed his words.

The woman could sense his hesitation and stopped for a second. Then she went to her suitcase and unzipped it. She pulled out a package that had been wrapped carefully in cloth, pushing it towards him. A stale-looking loaf of bread.

"I'm feeling a bit peckish. Would you like some?" Adam was flustered at this generosity. His gaze darted away from the woman, scanning for something worthy of reciprocating her gesture. All he could find were instant noodles and a can of tuna. He plugged in the electric kettle, and when the kettle spewed steam into the air, he poured the water into the cup of noodles. Spicy aromas wafted through the air, mingling with the smell of tuna. He tried to look for a tablecloth but could only find old newspapers. That would have to do. The two looked down at their feast sprawling across yesterday's front page: stale bread, instant noodles, and an opened can of tuna. There was only a single set of utensils. Without discussing it, the woman took the spoon, while Adam took the chopsticks. He found himself impressed by her appetite and dexterity. He started to move his chopsticks faster … he hadn't realized it, but he was hungry. He couldn't remember when he'd last had a proper meal with somebody.

While Adam chomped at his food, he imagined what this would look like. What a sight. Two strangers, silently sharing bread and fish, in the depths of the night.

The woman broke the silence, gently, as if she'd read his mind.

"You know, if you don't have anywhere to go, you can stay here while you look. Not for too long, just temporarily. What do you think?"

He couldn't fully grasp what she meant, but his stomach and heart both felt full enough for him to nod.

"I have some urgent errands to run tomorrow. Could you keep my stuff for me in the meantime?"

He happily nodded again.

The woman leaned back in relief. She stretched her arms and looked for a place to lay her head down. Adam looked around and started to pile a few books as if they were bricks. He gathered books of similar size to build pillars, then took a plank of wood he used as a desk to create a bedframe. This was his first official guest in his humble studio, and this was all he could offer. Sure, it was better than the cold concrete floor. Still, as Adam watched the woman lay contently on her bed of books – a crooked makeshift surface that was a disgrace to the idea of beds – his chest sunk with guilt. She turned her back towards him, assuming a fetal position. From behind she looked small, lonely, like she was a guest in a home in which she wasn't welcome.

As he usually did, Adam lay down on the futon. As the night grew darker, the rain fell more heavily. This night his studio was much louder than what he was used to, but he did not mind. The rhythm of raindrops, the howling notes of the wind, with the occasional tremor of another being's breath. Somehow, the noises came together and harmonized.

Again, he thought about the novel he had completed earlier in the day. He wondered if the woman had a life growing inside her, like she did in the novel. He stole a look at the woman. She snored loudly, seemingly exhausted by the events of the long day.

Adam tossed and turned, finding it difficult to sleep. It was astonishing that she could sleep so deeply, so carelessly. Sure, she'd traveled a long distance, but he was a stranger, a man she had never met. Sure, she was older and married, but he was a hot-blooded man in his prime. He felt himself stiffen. Perhaps it was anger, or resentment. Or perhaps it was just plain excitement from having a female in the studio.

The woman's snoring shifted to a sonorous, heavy breathing, like a lion exhaling in its slumber. The noise clashed against the downpour outside, as if she and the rain were competing to see who could be louder. The clock ticked. The darkness of the night deepened. And while she breathed, the rain continued to pour.

Adam's thoughts drifted back towards himself. It was odd how, in the midst of the present turmoil, he couldn't stop doting on the past. But then he turned to his side, telling himself the sun would still rise in the morning. Tomorrow's sun would shine brightly across his world. So tonight, at least in this moment, he could allow himself to live in the past.

Until the age of fifteen, he had lived in a shabby old house on the outskirts of the small city. Just he and his grandmother. He never knew his father. Mother had remarried when he was very young. Nevertheless, he was told that he was born into the world out of love, a beautiful ending to an exceptional, passionate love between soulmates. At least that's what he was told by his Grandma. Mother emigrated to a foreign country with her new family, so that was that.

He didn't really have hobbies or interests. Other than reading, of course. Reading transported him to new territories, strange lands that were far from his home. He dreamed of these faraway worlds, and he dreamed vividly. In fact, he was a superbly vivid dreamer. Almost prophetic, to the extent that people came to him when they had lost or were in search of certain things. They would drone on and on about their sad stories, boring him to sleep. Then he would dream for them. His reputation grew, and Grandma's friends from neighboring towns started coming to him for advice. It was fun at first, but then the dreams became too intense, and he quit. Dealing with the staring eyes was one thing, but he hated the idea of meddling with other people's lives.

It was around this time that he started talking in his sleep. He spoke loudly, enunciating words of a foreign language. Grandma wondered how he spoke in a language he had never learned. It didn't seem like anything she had heard in passing. She wanted to know what it was, so she asked a neighbor for help. The neighbor was a devout Christian, a worshiper of the Holy Spirit. It was frowned upon to invite a woman over to one's house in the middle of the night. It also didn't help that the neighbor's husband was delusional with jealousy. However, Grandma didn't give up. She waited for Adam to take a nap one day, took it as her chance, and ran to the neighbor. "Oi," she said casually, "I think my grandson has started to speak in tongues." The neighbor's eyes lit up, and she scurried back, excited to witness a divine gift. She stood over Adam as he napped, folded her hands in prayer and closed her eyes, whispering "O Lord, O Lord". They listened to him blabber in his sleep, trying to interpret the strange words that blended into a trance of snoring, breathing, sighs, and gasps. After a while, the neighbor shook her head and stepped back. It didn't sound like the Lord's tongues, she shrugged. Grandma begged, asking the neighbor to come by another time. It would be worth it, other days were different. She begged until the neighbor grew frustrated and lashed out, screeching that it must be Satan's work as she shut the door behind her.

Satan's work? How dare she! Grandma spat. My poor baby. He may not be my flesh and blood, but he's my darling baby boy, how dare she say such things. She cursed the door, and shivered. Until that moment, Adam was under the impression that Grandma was his father's mother. He's never considered the possibility that they might not be bonded by family. Grandma passed away when he turned fifteen, and once again he was orphaned. He never learned the truth. He drifted, from one odd job to the next. And he no longer had a home, but somehow managed to make ends meet. It wasn't as hard when one was alone. In the end he landed a job at the library, doubling as both the library's security and janitor. This was where he discovered books, and the joy of reading. He was hooked. He was home.

The sound of the rain heightened, suggesting that showers had become a storm. Raindrops banged against the concrete of the roof like the drumline of a marching band. Yet amidst the rhythmical thrumming of the rain there was something else, something very different. A stirring, amplified with each beat. The noise grew louder, sending shivers down Adam's spine.

P- … pl- … please …

It was coming from the woman, who still slept soundly. Adam glanced across at the woman. The noises became words.

Please, help me, save me. Please, mister.

Adam's eyes grew wide, full as the moon. Nobody had ever called him mister.

Nobody had ever asked him for help. In his entire life, nobody had ever, ever asked him to save them. He drew a little closer towards the woman, listening to her deep, lion-like breathing. He put his ear against her body.

What is it like out there, out in the world?

Adam realized where the voice was coming from. Mister, I want to know. The taste of life.

Oh yeah? Well, it tastes bitter, I can tell you that.

It floored him to think that somebody desired to see this bleak world so desperately.

What a disappointment it would be! One man's trash might be another's treasure, he supposed. Who was he to say his opinion was the truth? It wasn't like he was going to tell a brand-new soul at its purest that the world was jaded, materialistic, corrupt, unsalvageable, sinister even. He'd do no such thing.

The voice continued on like whispers in the wind.

Please, mister, would you stop my mother? Please? She's going to go to the clinic tomorrow morning. She thinks it's her choice, but don't I have a say in my life? Please convince my mother, please!

He closed his lips. There was a bitter taste in his mouth.

Lightning flashed outside, illuminating the room for a split second. The sound of thunder rumbled in the distance. Heavy rainfall sprayed the window. Adam curled like a caterpillar. The voice stopped whispering. Perhaps the thunder had frightened it into silence. The lightning and thunder weren't a coincidence, he told himself as he tried to put his unease to rest and remember the past, once again.

Perhaps he could raise the child as if it were his own. Grandma had done so for him.

It was possible.

The woman resumed her loud snoring, catching Adam off guard. He felt more awake than before.

Perhaps they could live together, he could live here with her. At least until the baby came. Was it even possible? He tilted his head. It was about time he did something brave. It was about time he stood up for himself, against the world. Especially if he wanted to be responsible for her. Responsible for the life inside of her. He nodded.

Although … why should he? It wasn't his child. It wasn't his place. He shook his head vigorously. He thought of the voice, the weak, desperate voice. He sat bolt upright. Tomorrow the sun would rise, and he would rise as well. Even if it were pouring rain, he would find something. There would be no job too small, no labor too intensive. He would find the way. A way to survive this brutal city. But was it that simple, or was he being naive? He shook his head, mumbling, now pacing left and right like a man trying to find his way through a maze.

Tears trickled down Adam's face. Not necessarily because of the memories from his youth. He didn't understand it, but he let the tears fall without wiping them away. He looked towards the woman through his tears. She was a blur, like a statue covered in a distant fog.

In the deep of the night, mist covered the rain-soaked city. In what seemed like a pitch black abyss, a new dawn was slowly awakening, preparing to bring forth and fill the skies with blindingly bright rays of sunlight.

*

Adam opened his eyes to the new morning's sunlight. Today was his twentieth birthday. The first thing he did as a twenty-year-old was to look around his studio. The woman was no longer there. He blinked, opening his eyes even wider, as if he'd missed something. But there was no one. He felt immediately lonely.

Was last night a dream? In the corner, the woman's suitcase suggested otherwise. A faint scent of spice and tuna hung in the air.

Adam felt a sharp pang in his chest. He hadn't relayed the message to her. He'd missed his chance. All because he stayed up too late.

He sat on the futon, pulling at his hair. He blamed it on his circumstances, how he had grown accustomed to staying up late working the night shift. He let out a long sigh. Then he reached for yesterday's novel, trying to remember and reconfirm.

Knock-knock at his door.

Adam froze, his hands still flipping through the pages. The knocking continued. He rose, and hesitantly poked his head out the door.

A male stranger, wearing a black vinyl raincoat. His scruffy face and unkempt hair sparked immediate suspicion. His face was expressionless, as if a ghost leered through the rain. Adam noticed a lump on his back under his raincoat. Perhaps he was deformed.

Perhaps he wore a backpack. Perhaps he was carrying a baby. It could be anything. The man met Adam's gaze, and pulled out a faded receipt, which he shoved in Adam's direction.

"Excuse me but is this the address shown here?"

Adam glanced at the receipt. "Yes, I believe so."

As soon as Adam's words left his mouth, he heard a loud thud. The man's expressionless face was now filled with rage, and he started to huff like a swordsman in battle. The man threw his raincoat on the ground, rolling up his sleeves. Adam could finally see what was on his back. It was no hump, no infant, not even a sword. It was a guitar. The man barked at Adam.

"There was a woman here, wasn't there?"

"Pardon, sir?"

Adam felt much more courteous than usual.

"What do you take me for, a fool? I know everything. Now open the damn door! Go on, open it!"

"Excuse me, sir. Sir! Hey now, just wait a minute"

Adam instinctively knew he was not to let the man in. He may not have been able to save the new life in the woman, but he could still protect her. Flames of righteousness and chivalry sparked in his heart. This part never happened in the novel, but anything could happen in this world.

Glaring at the man, Adam tightened his grip around the doorknob. He looked his adversary up and down. This bully was too tall, too brawny and, most of all, too eager to punch Adam in the face. He had a rather handsome face, Adam thought, wondering how he could be admiring his opponent at this moment. He probably leeched off the women that loved him, wooing them with his dashing eyes and long hair. Gold diggers weren't always women, after all. Adam cleared his throat.

"You've got a manly face. Seems like you couldn't man-up enough for your woman though."

He decided to leave out the part where the man was a scoundrel who took advantage of poor women.

"What did you say to me? Who the hell do you think you are?"

Adam's neck snapped forward as the stranger swiftly grabbed him by the collar.

Before he knew it, Adam was dragged out of his studio into the courtyard. The door swung wide open behind him to reveal, as if a gutted fish, the studio's insides. The woman's suitcase. The bed made of books, next to his futon. It was as if the curtain rose on a theater set.

"Well, well, well … what do we have here?"

The concrete courtyard was full of puddles from last night's rain. The man stomped through each and every puddle, as if he were crossing through a muddy swamp, dragging Adam out to the middle. As the men started to fight, water splashed in all directions, wetting any remaining part of the courtyard that had stayed dry. Through the scuffling, Adam caught a glimpse of the man's fist. It was coming straight at him.

Right at that moment, the woman returned to the courtyard. Her shoulders slumped helplessly.

"I knew it. Oi! Get your butt over here, right now!"

Holding a fist towards Adam, the man pointed at the woman with his other hand. His finger leveled at her as if he were aiming through a rifle scope. And his eyes lit up with fury. He was ready for battle. The woman looked back, unbothered. She walked past them without a word, as if she had seen nothing. She walked straight into the studio without a word. As if she were the owner of the house.

"What? Where are you going?"

The man stopped for a second, then returned his attention to Adam. He would take care of this weakling first. He growled like a beast, ready to feed on its prey.

"Oh, little pansy boy ... I knew from the beginning something was up."

Adam no longer had any courage left. This didn't happen in the novel. His life was no novel. He was having the worst luck today. He hunkered down, surrendering to his opponent.

But the man had lost his appetite to fight. Together with Adam, they trailed after the woman, a pair of zombies. There she stood, between the makeshift bed of books and messy futon. She spoke calmly.

"Could I bother you for a glass of water?"

Adam quickly fetched a large bottle. The woman popped open a jar of pills, revealing a multitude of tiny colored pellets. She took the bottle and knocked the pills back. Her nonchalance calmed Adam's nerves. In the novel, the man would get drunk and beat the woman. Now, in Adam's studio, in this reality, the man was gearing up for a fight, snarling like an animal. However, this time, the roles felt reversed.

The people in front of Adam were complete opposites of the characters in the novel.

It was odd how different they seemed. Adam felt conflicted, he felt confused. Did the words in the book not speak of truth? Was the novel lacking depth, only portraying generic images? Now that he was getting to know these two, Adam started to regret having being so impressed, so touched, by the novel.

"This is nothing like how it was supposed to be."

Adam muttered out loud, frustrated and more than a little bewildered. He looked at the two strangers in his studio, then down at his feet. The man and woman seemed to sense Adam's disappointment. Allowing a moment to pass, they started to orate loudly, like actors on a stage.

"Why did you leave like that? Without a word?"

The woman looked away, fiddling with the handle of her suitcase. She sniffled loudly.

Adam and the man looked at each other. An awkward silence filled the studio. Adam felt a hollow cavity form in his chest. Tears filled his eyes before he knew it.

"What about ... what about ...?"

The woman shook her head, parting her lips.

"I was ready ... ready to get rid of it ... I was on the table, but ... I couldn't do it. I just couldn't."

Adam opened his mouth, but only a hiccup came out. What he wanted to say was, you did good, you really did good. Instead, muffled hiccups filled the silence. The man stood in the corner, looking back and forth between Adam and the woman in utter confusion.

"Hey kid, you got a smoke?"

How crass of him to ask for cigarettes during such a moment. Adam sneered. And yet, he pulled from the back of his drawer a box of cigarettes that he'd been saving. The man lit up, and soon started to blow small smoke rings, one after the next.

Adam hiccupped. The man smoked. The clock ticked. The rings of smoke dissolved.

"Look, babe, look at me. I'm sorry. I really am. I'm nothing without you. I can't sing without you. Honey, do you hear me?"

The woman sniffled as the man spoke. Adam stared at them, wondering what the man's singing would sound like. Clearly, the woman had fallen in love with a voice, just as the novel had endlessly mentioned. He wanted to listen to this voice with his own ears.

"So, mister ... I hear you're quite the singer. Could you sing us something? For me? And for ... the child?"

The man's face softened, and he winked at Adam. Adam thought the wink was corny but, at the same time, somehow attractive.

The man reached for the guitar and cradled it carefully in his arms. He plucked at the strings with filthy long fingernails, tuning the guitar. Twang. Twwaaaang. Finally satisfied, the man closed his eyes. With each pluck, plink, and strum of the strings, somewhere above stars fell, a meteor shower across the night sky. Each note shone brightly, dazzling, filling the tiny room with wonder. The man opened his mouth. Those lips, that had not so long ago spat roughness, let out a gentle voice that flowed effortlessly like a river, carrying currents of sorrow and sweetness.

How could such a vulgar man have such a pristine voice? The man's voice and the song that it sang were celestial. Perhaps music wasn't simply a creation that belonged to man, but a gift that we borrowed from another world. Perhaps we were just vessels through which other beings played. Other greater beings that we would never learn of, from places that we would never hear of. Perhaps this was the case with everything that possessed beauty. Music, art, maybe even love.

Adam listened solemnly, feeling the hollowness in his chest well up with emotion.

The song concluded, and the man looked sheepishly towards the woman. "Come back to me, my love."

He spoke with softness, as if he were still in song. It was a cliché, but it worked. And it worked on Adam, too. The singer's cheesy words made the morning's havoc disappear, a cube of sugar melting into hot coffee.

How odd. The power that such words could possess.

They paused before him. "Goodbye." The woman with her suitcase, the man with his guitar. Then, as suddenly as they'd appeared, they vanished.

He replied quietly, bidding the couple goodbye. He bid the baby farewell.

Then once again he was alone. As if it had all been a dream. All he was left with were the piled books. He found the novel from the day before. It was damp from the rain, its pages curled now. He wondered when the book could have become so wet. Full of regret, he put the book aside and chose another from the pile.

Perhaps it was all a dream, a fantasy caused by being alone. Perhaps one day, knock-knock, someone else would come to his door, letting themselves into his life. Perhaps one day, he would dream alongside another being.

Adam leaned back on his futon, opening the first page of a new book.

SUE JA JOO

A novelist, poet, and playwright, Sue Ja Joo was born in Seoul, Korea. She emigrated in 1976, living abroad for 23 years in France, Switzerland, and the United States. She returned to Korea in 1998. Holding a B.A. in Fine Arts (Seoul National University) and an M.A. degree from Colgate Rochester Crozer Divinity School, Sue's literary inspiration comes from her deep roots in aesthetics, religion, and global cultures. In 2013, she became the first recipient of the Insung Park Mini-Fiction Literary Award, which recognizes her achievements in popularizing this genre in Korea. She is at the frontier of a new literary genre, 'Smart Fiction' which hybridizes poetry and short fiction. Sue is currently working as the editor-in-chief of a literary magazine based in Seoul. Sue Ja Joo lives in Korea.

About the Translator

Jennifer M. Cho is a Korean-American writer and translator. She has always been fascinated with the art of storytelling. Growing up in both Washington D.C. and Seoul, she found herself naturally drawn to the examination of communication and comprehension between different cultures and generations. After earning her degree in Digital Communication and Creative Writing from Stanford University, she pursued a career in video gaming—a platform for epic tales and sweeping sagas. She has worked in marketing and operations for global brands such as Electronic Arts, Sony PlayStation®, and NCsoft. Jennifer's interest shifted to the short communication form of the media industry. Working in advertising technology with mobile game studios across the world, Jennifer honed her skills in captivating audiences within a 15 to 30-second time frame.